MW01247529

Finding a Soul Mate

Meant to be Together, Volume 1

Richard Alan

Published by Village Drummer Fiction, 2019.

Dedication

This work would not have been possible without the love and encouragement of Carolynn Schwartz. She is my Bashert, my best friend, my lover, my partner, my wife, and the mother of our three boys. Long after we are gone, the walls of our home will still ring with her joyous laughter. Her disposition surrounds us with sunshine even on Seattle's cloudiest of days. I thank the Lord every day for putting Carolynn in my life.

This book is also dedicated to the memory of my mother, Sonya, who took me to a magical place called the library at a young age. I began my journey as a lifelong learner the summer of my fourth year, on a sunny day along the Mississippi River when we entered the Burlington Public Library in Iowa.

I also want to thank CJ Heck—poet, writer and teacher http://www.barkingspiderspoetry.com and Vietnam buddy Craig Latham, whose kind words about an article I wrote for CJ's blog, http://memoirsfromnam.blogspot.com/ encouraged me to start my writing career.

Lastly, I wish to dedicate this book to the memories of Daniel R. Hively, Robert Varick, Douglas S. Kempf, and all those brave men and women who did not make it home from Vietnam.

Prologue

TRADITION TELLS US that forty days before a male child is conceived, the name of his bride-to-be is announced from heaven.

There is a soul mate for everyone—however, not everyone finds his or her soul mate. We can spend our lives searching for our true soul mate. If we are one of the lucky ones, we find the match that was made in heaven just for us, the one we are meant to be with, and we will live a long, happy, and productive life together.

Bashert is a Yiddish word meaning *meant to be*. It goes beyond the coupling of two hearts destined for oneness, beyond two half-souls joined in completion.

I'm Meyer Minkowski and this is my story of love, life, and finding a partner.

Now, you have to understand, no one's life is just a single strand of thread. On the contrary, each of our lives are a tapestry, woven intricately with the lives of those with whom we cross paths and with whom we share history, destiny. In these pages you will find the strands that make up my tapestry.

Chapter One ~ The Wonder Years

FOLLOWING WORLD WAR II, it was difficult to earn a living in our small, Midwest Mississippi river town. During the summer between third and fourth grade, my family moved to a small suburb located east of Seattle, in the foothills of the Cascade Mountain range in Washington State. My father found a job working for the Boeing Company where his military experience as a crew chief was in demand.

Shortly after settling in to our new town, I was busy exploring my new neighborhood on my bicycle when someone yelled. "Hey, you!"

This was followed by a melodic laugh. I rode over to find a girl who was about my height with curly blonde hair, sparkling blue eyes, and an infectious smile.

"I'm Joan. I can show you everything in this town," she assured me.

While I was happy to find someone roughly my own age, I wasn't sure if I wanted to spend time with a girl.

Joan assured me it would be okay because her mother had declared, "Joan is the biggest tomboy in the county."

That was good enough for me.

Joan retrieved her bike and we rode off to find adventure. We peddled a couple of blocks into town and stopped at the back door of a bakery. Being a warm mid-July day, the door was open and a yeasty smell permeated the air. We parked our bikes and walked over.

Joan leaned into the doorway and shouted, "Hey Aldo."

"Hey, Joan. I be right out," I heard a deeply-accented voice reply.

The baker came out with his arms, hands, and apron dusted with flour.

"I see you have a new friend."

"His name is Meyer and he's from the same town where I used to live. I'm showing him around today."

Aldo shook my hand, transferring some flour to me. "Well if you kids are going to be riding around you going to need to keep your energy up." He disappeared into the bakery and returned with a six-inch loaf of French bread for each of us. It was still warm from the oven.

Mr. Aldo Theodorocopolis—it would be another year before I could pronounce his name and another two before I could spell it—warned us to look out for cars as we pedalled away.

There was a hobby shop in town. It was full of art supplies, toys, and model trains. I loved to visit and plan which railroad train cars I needed next, while Joan explored the art supplies.

My father built an eight-foot by eight-foot table for a train platform out of two four-by-eight sheets of plywood. He cut a hole in the middle where I would command my HO scale train empire.

The platform was in the corner so two walls were immediately next to it. Dad put poster board along those walls for me to paint background scenes. He had helped me with the track layout but then told me to do the scenery and buildings by myself, a little at a time. I started building scale structures, but couldn't paint anything that would pass for scenery and my attempts to paint the cars and structures were awful.

I told Joan about my inability to paint scenery for my railroad. I had been trying to create a mountain logging operation. She took my watercolor paints and starting painting the poster boards precisely as. Joan, I thought, could see what was in my mind.

My mother showed us how to make paper Mache mountains, tunnels, lakes, and rivers, which Joan painted. She added rocks from our gravel driveway depicting boulders in and around the paper Mache mountains. We found some paint called "grime" which Joan used to make some of the rail cars and buildings look weathered.

Any rainy day, or any day when we were tired of the heat of the Northwest summer, we would head down to the basement and work on our railroad. We agreed we would call it the Meyer-Joan Railroad, the MJ for short. Joan artfully lettered some of the box cars and an engine with the name.

I noticed on the left side of the cars she would print the Joan-Meyer Railroad and on the other side she would print the Meyer-Joan Railroad. As we were sharing everything on the train table, I thought the names were appropriate.

Occasionally, Joan would build a diorama at her house to add to the railroad table. My parents were amazed at her artwork. They invited her parents over one Friday night to see Joan's artistic talent. That's how Joan's parents met my parents and our families became good friends. We had Sabbath dinners at each other's homes the same way we did with some of my relatives.

• • • •

ONE WARM, SUNNY DAY, Joan showed me a little stream which wound through our neighborhood.

She told me we must look in the stream in the fall because big salmon would be returning from the ocean to the same stream and we might see them. I wasn't too impressed with her stream. I was used to seeing the mighty Mississippi River. Being new to the Northwest, I found it silly to think some big fish from the ocean could end up in this tiny little stream.

Joan showed me the little minnows in the stream. She pointed out how they travel in groups and asked me if I knew why they suddenly darted and then stayed still for a while.

"They're fish and that's what fish do," I told her. We both dropped down on our knees and peered into the clear water to get a better look.

"I know they're fish and I know what fish do," she said wistfully. Then she looked up at me. "But why?"

For the first time in my life I was hit by a vacuous feeling of not being able to explain something as simple as a minnow. "I was planting flower seeds at our new house. I covered them with dirt and I was wondering how they would know which way was up?"

"Yes," she exclaimed as she jumped up. "You get it!"

Within a couple of weeks of my arrival, the town librarian knew both our names and knew that each time we came we would have a question. She was always eager to help. Every visit, she taught us a little bit more about using the library as a tool to research any topic. By the end of the summer, the librarian had taught us how to use everything from the Dewey Decimal system to the Index of Periodic Literature. She even taught us how to make proper index cards on which to keep our information.

We spent the entire summer exploring the town plus our stream. We continued to ask each other questions. Being so young we didn't realize as we shared the exploration of our new Northwest environment, joked, and laughed together, we were also beginning to explore who we were.

· · · ·

WE OCCASIONALLY COLLECTED bottles and returned them for their deposit. One day, when we had two dollars saved up, we decided to go to the local Chinese takeout. At our respective homes we only received half of an eggroll when Chinese meals were served so we decided to buy a dozen and eat them all ourselves. Sitting in the middle of a tall grass-covered field on a sunny day, we stuffed ourselves with six eggrolls apiece. For the next three years I could not even look at an eggroll.

But something else happened as we consumed our eggrolls. For the first time in my life, I felt a connection to a person who wasn't a relative. To this day I can't describe our first connection, but I knew it existed.

We also tried hugging that summer. Joan told me her parents were always hugging and they seemed to enjoy it, so we should try. While we hugged each other, I remember thinking about a lamppost I had hugged recently during a game of hide and seek. We decided hugging was another thing we didn't know about but didn't care to know about.

I made lots of new friends once school started in the fall and occasionally saw Joan, but she was a year older and had older friends. Even so, at various times over the next few years, we used rainy days to continue building our railroad.

• • • •

THE NEXT SUMMER DURING August, my dad was in Chicago on business and the rest of us flew out to spend a few days with relatives. My parents decided our family would take the train back to the Northwest, as the train would pass through some of the most beautiful scenery in the country.

Joan's mom heard we were going to Chicago and she had asked my mom if we could bring Joan back to Washington State. Joan was spending the summer with cousins in Chicago and she didn't want her coming back on the train alone.

I was ecstatic to be on a train ride anywhere, especially a multiple day trip. We had seats in the Vista Dome car. It was the first passenger car on the train. The seats were arranged with two wide seats on each side of a center aisle. I sat next to a soldier in the row behind my parents.

We left Chicago in the early evening. As the conductor entered our car to take tickets, I had made some dumb remark about his skin color. I was repeating something one of my inconsiderate friends had said, but I certainly should have known better. Both my parents turned to slap me, and unfortunately for me, my dad's hand arrived at the side of my head first. Well, if I'd had eyes on my neck, I could have watched my head roll across the floor.

Sometime during the night, we were stopped in a train yard. I went back to the area between cars where the conductor had the door open and steps in place for passengers. He was a tall black man who stood straight as a soldier. His mostly black and white uniform was immaculate and I was sure I could see my reflection in his brilliantly polished shoes.

"They're going to switch engines here," he told me. "Do you want to watch?"

"Yes, sir," I practically screamed at him.

He told me to stand about ten feet from the side of the train, next to a steel beam supporting a canopy over the train. "Now you stay right there and you don't move until I tell you."

"Yes, sir."

The monster diesels that had pulled us from Chicago were replaced with a new set to pull us across the northern Rockies. I was entranced by the deep rumble of the powerful diesel engines and enjoyed the oily scent their exhaust wafted into the air. The engineer coupled the new engines into the train so gently, the passenger cars didn't move. Every time I glanced at the conductor he was watching me with a big smile. He called me and I raced back up the steps onto the train.

"Every trip, I get some young train enthusiast who gets to see the engine changeover. On this trip you were the lucky one."

"Yes, sir, I did get lucky and thank you *very* much."

I had just arrived back to my seat when the train started moving again. With the gentle rocking motion, I was soon fast asleep. When I woke up the next day, we had finished crossing the plains and I could see mountains in the distance. I was fascinated watching from the Vista Dome car as the train started to wind its way into the

Rocky Mountains. From our elevated position I could see both ends of the train, especially on turns.

Joan spent a lot of time the first morning playing with my sister, who is five years younger than me. After lunch she was put down for a nap and Joan came up to the Vista Dome. My dad was next to me and I had the window seat. Joan and I were kneeling side by side on the seat, with our faces plastered against the window, looking at the amazing scenery. Even the train-geek in me had to admit the scenery was gorgeous.

Joan was concentrating so hard, I believed she was trying to memorize every detail of the beauty passing in front of her. The further the train traveled into the mountains, the more picturesque the scenery became. Every bend brought new sights.

At one point, we travelled next to a broad mountain stream whose choppy surface reflected points of sunlight appearing as brilliant diamonds set into the surface of the water. As we passed one particularly flat section of the mountain stream, I noticed many silver rocks just under the surface. As I watched, I was shocked when the rocks started moving.

"Probably trout," my father said.

"Wow," said Joan. "This is great."

From snowcapped mountains in the distance to huge stands of evergreens, Joan and I discussed every detail.

About three thirty in the afternoon my dad gave us each a ticket for a sundae and told us to go to the dining car where there was a counter for serving snacks and ice cream. We raced there and found a couple of stools.

"Welcome to my dining car a neatly uniformed man said. What can I prepare for you?"

Joan said, "I'd like a sundae, please."

"Thank you, miss," replied the waiter as Joan passed him her ticket.

"And what would you like, sir?" I replied I wanted a sundae as well.

"Thank you, sir," he told me, taking my ticket. He placed a long silver spoon on a neatly folded cloth napkin in front of each one of us. He paused for a moment and asked, "Would you prefer a *he* sundae or a *she* sundae?"

We'd never heard of them before, but I asked for a *he* sundae and Joan asked for the *she* sundae. He talked to us in such a polite manner and exhibited such professional demeanour, it made me sit up straight and try to be on my best behavior.

Each sundae arrived in a lovely stemmed, pewter dish, topped with whipped cream. Mine had pieces of fresh pineapple on top and Joan's had fresh dark cherries. I immediately reached for my spoon, but before I could dig in, the waiter said quietly, "Sir." He looked down at my still-folded napkin.

I quickly put the napkin on my lap and then as neatly as possible attacked the sundae. The dark chocolate fudge running down the side of the vanilla ice cream was not as sweet as the chocolate bars I was accustomed to. However, the slightly bitter taste of the fudge contrasted with the sweetness of the ice cream. The fresh pineapple slices exhibited their usual ability to be sweet and tart at the same time.

As we ate, we asked the waiter what was he enjoyed most about the train.

"I love to see the herds of elk, deer, buffalo, and the occasional bear, but the nights in the mountains are the best." He stopped drying a glass and closed his eyes for a bit, then turned to us and said, "The clear night sky has more stars and constellations than any man can count."

My dad came into the dining car with my little sister and they sat next to us. He asked the waiter how Joan and I were behaving. "Your children have impeccable manners, sir," the waiter told him. Dad told Joan and me that he was proud of our "impeccable" manners.

I was fairly certain impeccable was better than good and might even have been better than great.

Most people abandoned the Vista Dome, as soon as the sky began to darken. That was sad, as the night sky, as the purveyor of our ice cream reported, consisted of a panorama of stars. My parents called Joan and me back to our seats and told us to go to sleep. I awoke about two in the morning and decided to check out the view from the Vista Dome. I took my blanket with me as the high mountain air had cooled off the interior of the train.

When I arrived at the front seat I saw someone already there. It was Joan, who had also decided to see if the waiter was right about the night sky. We wrapped ourselves in our respective blankets. We must have appeared to be a couple of youngsters trapped in cocoons with only our faces showing. We lay on our backs and looked out through the Vista Dome's glass panelled ceiling.

We thought we saw Orion, the North Star, the Big and Little Dippers, the Seven Sisters, and Venus. In the morning my mom found us still sound asleep. She woke us and told Joan to get cleaned up and dressed because she would be getting off the train right after breakfast to meet her parents.

I said good-bye to her after breakfast and ran up to the Vista Dome. I saw my mom and Joan meet Joan's family on the station platform in Everett, Washington. There were hugs all around. As Joan and her family turned to leave, Joan looked up to the front of the Vista Dome car and waved to me. I waved back and soon the train was on its way again.

• • • •

EVERY DAY DURING FIFTH grade, my best friend, Tim, and I would walk together to school and home. After school on Tuesdays and Thursdays, we would walk into the center of town, as I was going to Hebrew school and Tim was going to Catechism. The Synagogue was a block further than the church so it made sense for us to walk together. One day we were goofing around and arrived at the Church about twenty minutes late. Father Hanrahan was standing in the doorway waiting for us.

"Aren't you going to be late for Hebrew School, Meyer?"

"Yes, Father," I told him and took off running.

As I arrived at Hebrew School, Rabbi Hirschman's countenance left little doubt I was in big trouble. "I understand you made your friend Tim late for Catechism today. I expect a minimum paper from you in no more than two days, on the Jewish value of friendship and how we use those values to show our respect for our friends. And believe me; making them late for their religious duties is not one of them."

When I arrived home the look on my parents' faces told me they had heard from the Rabbi and I was in deep trouble.

While walking to school the next morning Tim told me, "We can't be late for religious classes again. My parents almost killed me for making you late for Hebrew school and Father Hanrahan has me writing a paper on the Christian value of friendship."

• • • •

IT WASN'T UNTIL A SCHOOL dance during the spring of seventh grade I had a chance to have much interaction with Joan again. Karen O'Reilly had begged me to be her date for the dance, which I ultimately agreed to do. At the dance it became obvious she wanted to go with me so she could be close to my best friend, Tim. I ended up alone standing in a corner, feeling much the village idiot.

I noticed Joan and some guy were having an argument. It ended with a few obscenities on the guy's part and tears running down Joan's face. The guy and his buddies were laughing at her as they walked away. She wasn't far from where I was standing and she looked in my direction, shrugged her shoulders, and used the back of her hand to wipe away a tear.

I approached her. "He doesn't want to know why minnows do what they do." She tried to manage a smile.

Summoning up all my seventh-grade male charm and debonair manner, not to mention courage, I informed her, "A hummingbird's heart beats two hundred fifty times a minute when it is resting and twelve hundred beats per minute when it's feeding."

She stared at me for a moment and then laughed her wonderful melodic laugh. We talked and joked for a bit and then, after summoning up more courage, I asked her to dance. She agreed and we enjoyed our first dance.

Junior-high dances mostly played fast dance music with an occasional slow song. Joan and I had danced five fast dances when a slow one began. I was hesitant because only couples who were going steady danced slow dances together. As the music began, I held out my hand out to Joan, she took it and we started our first slow dance together.

As I held her against me, it occurred to me this felt much different from the little girl who reminded me of a lamppost when we hugged. Joan was soft in places not even in existence a few years ago. As we danced, the feeling of having a special connection to someone came back to me, but it was different this time.

Joan put her head on my shoulder with her face close to mine, but not touching. Even so, I felt the warmth from her cheek. She gently sighed, placed her cheek firmly against mine, and slipped her hand around the back of my neck.

Somehow this was different from the other times I had danced slowly. As we moved, wrapped around each other, I began experiencing a feeling from deep inside me I wanted to protect her.

There I was, this thin seventh grader who probably couldn't punch his way out of a paper bag, suddenly entertaining thoughts that if Joan and I had to get out of a paper bag, I would somehow lead the way out.

That fall, Joan went off to high school and I was a busy eighth grader. I saw her around the neighborhood a few times, but other than an occasional hello, I only talked to her when she attended my school's performance of "Oklahoma" in which I was one of the leads. She told me I was a great actor and should try out for some of the plays when I arrived in high school.

Chapter Two ~ The Cabin

HIGH SCHOOL WAS THE worst four years of my life. I wouldn't know why until many years later. I couldn't concentrate as long as the other kids. With the exception of Algebra and Geometry, my grades were terrible.

I also experienced mood swings, resulting in my getting extremely angry over minor incidents. This rarely resulted in a physical outburst. I could reduce a girl to tears, or lose a guy friend, in a handful of choice insults thanks to the huge vocabulary I had from all my reading. My best friend once told me, behind my back I was known as the "Lone Ranger of Character Assassination."

The worst physical harm I endured in high school was when I tried to separate two girls who were fighting over my friend, Tim. Both girls were in the group of friends I ran around with during high school. As I tried to separate them, one of them hit me on the head with her clutch bag. I swear she must have had a brick in it. As the room started spinning, I saw stars.

One of my fellow drummers saw my predicament and pulled me away from the two fighting females. I had a throbbing headache all the rest of the day and a lump on my head I was sure was the size of Nebraska.

Joan saw me later in the day with an ice bag on my head so I related why I needed it. She advised me, in no uncertain terms, "Do not ever do something as stupid as trying to separate two girls who are fighting over a guy."

Throughout high school, Joan and I remained friends. I had a few girlfriends and Joan had a few boyfriends, but other than a couple trips to the art museum, we never dated each other.

After Joan completed high school, she worked as a nanny for a year to save money for college. I had been desperately looking for a summer job. The only thing I could find was a part time job washing dishes at a restaurant for fifty dollars per week.

A day before summer vacation began I received a phone call from the owner of the farm where Joan worked. Joan told him that I was looking for work, and he was looking for summer help. He needed someone for about four hours each day for mowing, taking care of his vegetable garden, and tending to the flower gardens around the house.

"It's going to be hot and sweaty work," he told me.

Suddenly washing dishes in a restaurant wasn't such a bad idea, until he said he would pay me a hundred and ten dollars per week. I knew I could handle hot and sweaty for that princely sum so I rode my bike the seven miles out to the farm and met Mr. Horner in person.

He told me he and his wife usually took care of the gardens, but he had a lot of debt this year and they were going to take factory jobs for a few months until they were caught up.

Each day I rode my bike out to the farm. I mowed, weeded, or completed a list of chores. I arrived at sunup each morning and finished by mid-afternoon.

Most days I brought a lunch and ate with Joan and the Horner's little kids. They adored Joan. She would read to them, play games, and teach them songs. While the kids napped mid-afternoon, Joan and I would sit on the big porch swing. We would talk and read for a couple of hours before I'd head home. With all the work, my body lost nearly all its fat and I was in excellent physical condition.

Our jobs at the farm lasted until the end of August and the Horner's had enough money put away to quit their factory jobs. Mr. Horner was relieved to get back to his farm and leave, what he called, "the mind-numbingly boring assembly-line work."

Shortly before I went to college, Joan told me we could drive up to northern central Washington State and use her family's A-frame cabin for a week. Her parents weren't too happy with just the two of us spending a week there, but thought it was better than Joan being at the cabin alone. Joan sternly informed me, "The cabin has two separate bedrooms, and we will be sleeping separately."

"There's no TV so we should bring lots of reading material," Joan warned. "Also there's a shooting range nearby, so you can bring your rifle and teach me how to shoot."

Oh wow! I had just received a Remington Model 700 rifle—7mm Remington Magnum caliber— as a graduation present. It was suitable for hunting any large animal in North America. My friend Gene, and I had just zeroed the sight a few weeks prior. I would also take a .22 rifle for Joan to learn on since the 7mm had too big a kick for a beginner.

We left early on Saturday morning so we would complete the four-hour drive before noon. I was allowed to take my father's 1961 Corvette. As my dad watched me drive away, I had the feeling his main concern was my taking good care of the car, rather than the fact Joan and I were spending a week together in a cabin.

As I pulled onto I90 and headed into the Cascade Mountain Range, I was tempted to open up the Corvette to show off for Joan, but a certain feeling was creeping back into my life. I tried to ignore it at first, but it was there whether I liked it or not. It was that old feeling in my gut that I wanted to be Joan's fearless protector. For the first time in my life, I drove a powerful sports car well within its limits and as smoothly as possible.

As we cruised, Joan and I started talking about the Vietnam War, but then it was laughing and joking with each other over the roar of the wind coming into the Corvette. I preferred the top up to avoid the sun, but Joan wanted it down to feel the wind in her hair and to see all the scenery during the drive—it was a breathtaking ride through the Cascade Mountain Range, many of whose peaks were snow covered.

After leaving the interstate we started into north central Washington's mountains and forests. We cruised through the town of Cashmere and Joan noticed a farmer's market. I wanted to keep driving, but Joan insisted we stop, "just to see what they were selling."

It was a bountiful display and we loaded up on local nectarines, peaches, apricots, apples, zucchini—and zucchini flowers, oddly enough—various fresh vegetables, plus fresh herbs and garlic. Joan picked up flowers to "beautify the cabin."

The next part of our drive took us along the broad, swift moving Columbia River. Joan was radiant as each new panorama came into view. We talked and debated many topics along the drive, but our conversation was regularly interrupted by Joan's shouts of delight as she directed my attention to yet another gorgeous view.

We laughed a lot, and with each golden peal of Joan's melodic laughter, I felt closer to her. A few times I interrupted our high-speed cruise, to take pictures for her.

As we stopped at yet another scenic view, I tried to tease her. "You've been up here many times before and you still get excited to see all this again?"

She shrugged. "I guess I'm wired that way. It's truly as beautiful and amazing to me as the first time I saw it—it's more special this time, because I get to share the beauty with someone else."

Joan gazed up at me with those incredible sparkling, blue eyes and took my hands in hers. "I knew I wanted to share this with someone crazy. Someone crazy who was willing to spend time with me kneeling by the side of a stream looking for minnows."

I knew it was supposed to be a platonic week, but I couldn't help myself. I wrapped my arms around her, pulled her tight against me. She stood on her toes and kissed my cheek.

"I'm so glad you were willing to come with me. I've been thinking about it all summer and it would have been sad if you weren't able to join me. According to my mom, being able to share scenery like this makes the experience better."

"I'd say she's right."

As we drove out of the mountains and into a wide valley, we were greeted by deep blue Lake Chelan. The lake is a pristine, glacier-fed body of water, fifty miles long and one and a half miles wide at its widest and over one thousand feet deep at its deepest.

The surface was cluttered with motor boats, water skiers, and sailboats. The lake begged us to dive into its clear waters on this hot August day. We stopped a few more times for pictures and then at a small grocery store where we bought sufficient provisions for our first few days at the cabin. The little Corvette had so much stuff in it, poor Joan had to have the last two bags of groceries in her lap for the fifteen-minute drive up the gravel road to the cabin.

The cabin was located on the side of a mountain with magnificent views. The shimmering blue of Lake Chelan, seen from our lofty perch, was quite a contrast to the intense green of the surrounding farms and forest-covered mountains. The cabin itself was a small A-frame with two bedrooms in the rear upper half of the unit, and a kitchen and bathroom below the bedrooms.

The interior front of the cabin was completely window covered from the floor to the steep sides of the A-frame's roof; the view only interrupted by the centrally located stone covered fireplace. A wide deck on the front of the cabin had enough furniture for *al fresco* dining plus a wide porch swing, some simple chairs, and a lovely hand-hewn railing around the deck edge. Various trails led away from the cabin and around the forty-acre property.

We unloaded all the groceries and luggage and stored them in the cabin. I opened windows to let in some fresh air while Joan found vases for the flowers and placed them around the cabin.

I was hanging clothes in my bedroom when Joan called to me to say she was going out to look for berries on the trail leading away from the front of the cabin. There was a hundred-yard-long tangle of raspberry bushes dotted with bright red berries about twenty-five yards in front of the cabin.

I walked onto the front deck and spotted Joan just off the trail near the first group of bushes. She was putting berries in a large colander. I was admiring her cream-colored skin, when out of the corner of my eye I noticed a large black bear enjoying the same row of raspberry bushes. It was fifty yards away from Joan and hadn't seemed to notice her.

I briefly thought about yelling to alert her, but realized I might also alert the bear to her presence. Instead, I quickly ducked into the cabin and retrieved my new rifle. I ripped open a box of cartridges and just as I started loading them into the rifle, I heard Joan's blood-curdling yell.

My pulse began racing as I rapidly stuffed a handful of extra rounds in my pants pocket while running onto the deck. I saw Joan trip and fall as she started up the trail from the bushes.

The bear, running now, was not far behind her. I raised the rifle to my shoulder, and with Gene's marksmanship advice echoing through my head, I calmly and carefully sighted the cross hairs at the bear's shoulder and squeezed the trigger. The rifle's booming sound echoed throughout the surrounding forest. I immediately racked the bolt and chambered another round in case I needed to shoot again. Looking through the scope, I saw the 7mm Magnum round had done its job. I clicked the rifle's safety on and took off running down the trail toward Joan.

She was trying to stand.

"You okay?" I asked.

"Twisted my ankle. It hurts like hell."

"Let me help you." I put my arm around her waist and helped her back inside. "I should call the Sheriff and tell them what happened."

"Hold me first, please."

Putting the rifle down, I held her, Joan's face buried against my neck and her arms around me, while she cried.

Without letting go of me she looked up smiling. "I always pick berries in the summer when we come here—I've done it a thousand times by myself. The one time I'm in great danger, there you were. The moment I saw you on the deck with the rifle against your shoulder, I knew you were going to do whatever it took to protect me. And you did."

She started kissing me but when she put weight on her twisted ankle, she groaned in pain.

I helped her to a chair.

"I'll get some ice to put on your ankle."

I called the Sheriff's office and they said they would be right there. It turns out they had been worried about this bear, as it was losing its fear of humans and was believed to be responsible for mauling some hikers a month before.

"We tried moving it some distance away last year, but it found its way back," he told us. They were grateful for my actions, and as regrettable as the animal's death was, they agreed it was the only option.

• • • •

I MADE DINNER FOR US so Joan could stay off her sore ankle. Afterward, we went onto the deck and read together on the porch swing. Joan insisted on positioning us in a way so we were touching each other, even if it meant only our feet were touching.

When it was too dark to read outside, we went in and sat in front of the fireplace. All the cabin lights were off so the only light was from the burning logs. I sat on the floor with my back against a big chair while Joan sat between my legs leaning against me.

As we bathed in the light and warmth of the fire, enjoying each other's warmth as well, I had one arm wrapped around her abdomen.

She took my hand and pushed it under her shirt and onto her breast. I remembered during dinner, thinking her breasts seemed to jiggle more than usual, but my still somewhat adolescent mind only now realized she wasn't wearing a bra.

I wrapped my other arm around her so I had both breasts in my hands. She sighed and wrapped her arms over mine to hold them in place while I caressed her.

After a while we took off our shirts and Joan turned around, wrapping her arms and legs around me, so she could sit on my lap facing me. We inspected every inch of each other's upper bodies.

It had started to rain slightly and we could hear thunder in the distance, which only increased the romance of the moment. Joan told me her older sister had told her how to give a guy a hand job.

"Do you want me to do it for you?" she asked.

I wasn't too sure, but since she couldn't get pregnant from a hand job, I thought, what the heck. I undid my belt and unbuttoned the top button of my shorts then Joan lowered my zipper and slid her hand onto me.

Hello—did that feel great.

I had done it myself any number of times, but this, this was far superior. With a little guidance from me, she was able to complete the act. Unfortunately *the act* was now flowing down her belly, but she just giggled, grabbed her shirt, and with a casual swipe it was gone.

"Thank you. Thank you," I said.

She smiled. "Thank you for letting me."

"What about you? Don't you want me to do the same for you?"

She looked at me for a bit, and then, grinning, she nodded her head and opened her shorts. She guided my hand to the place she wanted me to touch. "There. Just move your fingers a little bit sideways when you touch me there. Yes, just like that." She moaned a couple of times and then began kissing me. After a while she held me tightly while her beautiful body convulsed against me.

Afterwards, we held each other, talking and listening to the increasing sound of the thunder as it came closer. We decided to go to bed, and as I walked up the stairs behind her to help, I noticed her ankle seemed much better.

At the top of the stairs Joan turned to me. "Thunder frightens me, so I think we should sleep together."

Now who could possibly argue with Joan's incredible logic? Not I.

She slid into bed facing me and gave me a long kiss goodnight. Lying on my side, I pulled the big blankets over us as Joan turned away and pushed herself up against me. I wrapped my arm around her waist, but she pulled it up until I was cupping her breast.

"Hold me this way," she insisted. I fell asleep listening to the crackle of the dying fire and the sound of Joan's gentle breathing. We slept the whole night curled around each other.

The next morning we went to the shooting range so I could begin teaching her how to use firearms.

"Next time, I'll save you," she insisted.

Joan was an excellent student and did exactly what I taught her. She followed every bit of safety advice, to the letter. As a result, she did well and we had a lot of fun. On the drive back to the cabin she told me she couldn't wait to go shooting again.

After lunch we decided to head out for a brief hike around the property so Joan put on tall hunting boots to protect her ankle. As soon as we left the cabin, a few clouds appeared. They were a relief from the intense heat the sun generated during the previous day's cloudless sky.

We spent a few hours hiking into heavily forested areas, listening to the bird calls and the sound of the wind in the tops of the evergreens. On our return the clouds thickened as we approached our temporary home. The cabin was only a couple of hundred yards away when I felt something strike the top of my head. I looked behind to see if Joan had thrown something but she was bent over studying wildflowers, not looking in my direction.

I reached up to my head and realized I had been hit with a rain drop. I looked to the west and saw a wall of water was coming at us. Pointing at the rain, I yelled to Joan to head for the cabin. With her sore ankle she couldn't run. Sheets of acorn-sized raindrops fell on us. When the first drops hit the dirt road, the dirt puffed up into the air as if I had thrown a rock at it. Within a few seconds the dust was turned to sticky mud. In addition, the temperature dropped quickly. By the time we arrived back to the cabin, we were completely soaked and shivering.

Once inside, I quickly built a fire and Joan closed the drapes on the front windows so we could undress and warm ourselves in front of the fireplace. I carefully removed the large boot from Joan's sore ankle. She arranged all our wet clothes in front of the fire to dry. I brought us some towels and we took turns toweling off each other.

We tried to embrace but Joan couldn't get her hips against mine as my excitement was in the way. She pushed it down slightly and slid it between her legs without it being inside her. She whispered in my ear. "My mom had me start on the pill last month so I would be ready for college life. We can go all the way without my getting pregnant."

As she was sliding her hips up and back on my sensitive part, I once again discovered I couldn't find any reason to argue with her brilliant logic. We decided I would sit on the big rug in front of the fireplace and Joan would sit on my lap facing me. With Joan on top, she could control how fast she wanted to take me inside her. As she slowly lowered herself onto me, she had an uncomfortable look on her face.

"If it hurts too much, we should stop."

"No! It hurts like hell, but it feels so much better than it hurts."

We stayed still for a while with me completely inside her and then we slowly started to move. I knew enough about sex to know to wait for her to finish first, but knowing and doing are two different things. Instead of concentrating on what we were doing, I tried to stay calm by thinking about the throw-out bearing we were going to repair on my buddy's hot rod. Then I tried doing addition in my head...then long division...then multiplying polynomials. For heaven's sake, if someone could see inside my head they would have thought I was competing in a math contest, not participating in the world's most beautiful act with one of the world's most beautiful women!

I was just starting to simplify complex fractions when Joan's breathing became faster and her body started to shudder. I felt her muscles tightening on me. Feeling her body's signal, I finished.

"My lord," she said. "You made me feel...so...that was beautiful."

We held each other for quite a while and then took a warm shower together.

We dressed and returned to the warmth of the fireplace to read. I was on the floor on my side. After reading for a while Joan put a pillow on my hip, wrapped her arms around my legs, and fell asleep. She woke after a couple of hours, and smiling at me, said we should make dinner.

She prepared *radiatori* pasta while I chopped Roma tomatoes, crushed a clove of garlic, and shredded fresh mozzarella. Joan tossed them together with the warm pasta. She added the fresh basil and dried oregano we purchased from the farmer's market. Joan prepared the pasta so it retained enough warmth to melt the mozzarella, gently warm the tomatoes, and bring out the fragrant aroma of the garlic and herbs. She also sautéed zucchini flowers in butter and olive oil. Next she poured a small amount of rosemary infused olive oil over each plate of pasta.

After eating some of each, I said, "Now I know the meaning of the phrase—food for the gods." Her sparkling blue eyes stared at me for a bit while she maintained a blank expression. Tears were formed in her eyes. Just as I was thinking she was upset with me, she jumped up, came over, and kissed me.

She sat on my lap and told me, "I feel so good and secure when you're with me, when your arms are holding me, and especially when you're inside me."

I was young then and didn't understand the depth of feeling she had for me. I did know for the first time, when Joan's life was at stake, I had the knowledge and practiced ability to protect her. That gave me more joy than almost anything else in my young life.

Over the next few days we did many of the touristy things in the Lake Chelan area. We went down to the lake for swimming and boating, and we explored the many unique stores. We interspersed those activities with hurried rushes back to the cabin to "help each other," as we began to call making love. And we laughed, teased, and read to each other. We debated politics, the merits of the Vietnam War, pollution control, and topics of the day. I am sure the cabin, if it still exists, continues to ring with the sound of Joan's melodious laughter.

On Friday morning we slept in, packed a picnic lunch, and hiked to a nearby mountain top. We ate on a grassy knoll overlooking the wide valley with a beautiful mountain range in the distance. Late in the afternoon we headed back to the cabin for more reading, debating, and laughing.

As it was Friday, we prepared to celebrate the Sabbath. We both showered and put on the traditional Israeli attire of white shorts and shirts. Always thoughtful, Joan brought Sabbath candles from home for us. I brought out the little prayer books my family used on Friday nights. Joan recited the blessing for lighting the candles. She was radiant. The glow from the candles illuminated her hands, as she held them covering her face while she chanted the blessing.

We wished each other a "Good *Shabbos*" then embraced. I held up a glass of wine...really grape juice—and recited the blessing over the "fruit of the vine." We each took a sip.

Joan placed a pitcher of water at the kitchen sink so we could do the ritual washing of our hands prior to her blessing the *Challah* she baked for us. We sang *Shalom Aleichem*, which means "Peace Unto You", then sat down to the oregano chicken dinner we had prepared.

All of our young years, we complained about going to synagogue, how boring it was, never seeing the significance of the Sabbath. But the first time we're alone together, we both wanted to honor the Sabbath and celebrate it properly. That first Sabbath we celebrated as a couple, would cement a connection between us which would last through our separation during our college years and my army years.

On Saturday we spent the day studying, reading, and "taking care of" each other. Saturday evening we went into town for dinner at a restaurant, went for a walk along the lake, and then headed back up the mountain.

Early Sunday morning we went through the cabin and cleaned it up one last time. As we drove away, I glanced in my rear-view mirror and felt a twinge of sadness because the cabin had returned to being an empty wooden structure instead of being our love and laughter filled temporary home.

The ride home was as beautiful as the ride out, but the closer Joan and I were to our homes, the quieter we became.

"Back to our real lives," I said.

"I know. You're going to school in Florida and I'm going to school in Wisconsin."

"Maybe we should write. I think this has been the best time I've ever experienced."

She didn't reply. I was quiet for a while and then asked her, "Do you believe in *Bashert*?"

"I didn't before, but now I'm beginning to wonder. I can't stop feeling we're meant to be together. If we are, the Lord will put us together again." She kissed my cheek.

I quickly drove away after I dropped her off at her parents' house so she wouldn't see the tears in my eyes. A week later, I was on my way to Florida.

Chapter Three ~ Joan's Struggles

AT SCHOOL IN WISCONSIN, Joan made many new friends—bright people, most of whom were excited to be there, and who looked forward to the educational opportunities ahead of them.

Tommy was the son of a Nobel Prize winning physicist. He was intelligent, about five feet tall, somewhat chubby, and usually drunk on weekends. He'd asked her out a number of times but she'd always turned him down. Joan wasn't interested in someone who was so shallow he thought of heavy drinking as a manly accomplishment.

She was on her second date with a guy from one of her art classes. He was easy to spend time with. They had just met up with some of Joan's dorm-mates and their friends at a dance club.

They hadn't been there long when she heard a voice say, "Hey Joan. You bitch! You go out with him, but won't go out with me?"

It was Tommy and he was drunk to the point he was wobbling as he approached. She glanced at him and turned back to her date. Tommy grabbed her arm, spun her around, and slapped her.

Her cheek stung from the blow. Joan stepped back and realized her date was backing up quicker than she was. Tommy came toward her again with fury in his eyes, but Joan replaced it with a look of surprise and pain as she threw a fist into his midsection knocking the wind out of him, just the way her dad taught her.

A couple of bouncers arrived and asked if she was okay. She told them she was. They moved a thoroughly chastened Tommy through the crowd and out the front door without his feet ever touching the ground.

With one hand rubbing her cheek, she turned to her date. "Were you just going to stand there while he hit me again?"

"I am a non-violent person. I know violence only begets more violence."

"What if he had attacked you? Would you have resisted?"

"I would not have resisted physically but I can passively resist any man."

At that moment, Joan couldn't even remember what she had seen in this fellow in the first place. "I realized some time ago you had a big ass, but it's only now I've realized you do your thinking with that part of your anatomy." She turned and walked away, leaving him surrounded by his friends who were trying to stifle their laughter.

Joan and her roommate decided they'd had enough social interaction for the evening and walked back to their dorm together. Joan didn't really mind not having a boyfriend because she was still living in the glow Meyer and she had created during their week at the cabin.

As the glow faded, however, she started to feel lonely. A few weeks winter session started, she received a message to call her grandmother, Esther.

This can't be good news, she thought. She called her grandmother.

"I'm sorry to have to tell you this Joan, your parents and sister Golda, were in a terrible car accident. They're all in terrible shape. They were hit by a drunk driver who ran a stop sign. I have a plane ticket waiting for you at the airport, so get there as quickly as you can."

"I'll leave now, Grandma." *This can't be happening. Events like this happen to other people—not to my family.*

Joan quickly packed a bag. As she rode to the airport, she must have been crying as the cab driver repeatedly asked her if she was all right. Truthfully, she was experiencing such emotional turmoil, Joan was lucky to know up from down.

"I just need to get to the airport," she kept telling the driver.

She whimpered waiting for her flight and she cried her way across the country. During a stopover in Denver, she called her grandma.

"How are they doing, Grandma?"

"Just come home, Joan. I'll meet you at the airport," she replied with an exhausted tone in her voice. "I love you, dear."

Her grandma was right. Joan didn't really want to hear dreadful news over the phone, especially being so far away. She wondered if someone died.

What if my mom was gone? She and her mom had huge fights over the summer. After Joan arrived home from her trip to Lake Chelan, her mother nagged happy Joan concerning her relationship with Meyer.

"When he goes to college, he's going to major in mathematics. What kind of a living does a math teacher make?"

"He's the kindest boy I know and makes me happy."

Her mother screamed, "Are you crazy? Kind doesn't pay the bills."

The argument escalated and they'd ended up saying awful things to each other—terrible things a mother and daughter should never say. If anything happened to her now, Joan would never have the chance to apologize for her disgusting behavior.

What if my dad was gone? Her father was the light of Joan's life. When things became bad at home between Joan, her sister and her mother, he would patiently talk to them until they put their relationships back together. He understood how Meyer made Joan feel.

Joan knew this because it was her father who had convinced her mother, reluctantly, to agree to let her go to the cabin with Meyer.

What if my sister was gone? Her sister, Golda, had just become engaged to a wonderful man. It can't end this way for her.

What if both my parents were gone? They recently purchased a retirement home in Arizona and were counting the days until they could spend the rest of their lives in the warm Arizona sunshine.

Joan pushed the thought of losing all three of them out of her mind as it was simply too painful to contemplate.

As she stepped off the plane, she looked for her grandmother. Instead, Meyer's parents, the Minkowski's, were waiting for her. Mr. Minkowski had a stoic look expression and Mrs. Minkowski had red eyes and tears streaming down her cheeks. As Joan walked up to them, her whole body started trembling.

Mr. Minkowski spoke first. "I'm sorry to have to tell you this. Your dad died at the scene of the accident and your mom died a few hours ago." His voice sounded tight and controlled. "Your sister is in critical condition. The doctors don't know if she will survive the next twenty-four hours."

"No!" Joan screamed. "Don't tell me that. This can't be happening." She started sobbing uncontrollably. Her whole body was shaking and she could feel her legs getting weak. The room started to spin.

Mr. Minkowski grabbed her just as she was collapsing. He and his wife helped her over to a bench and sat with her until the airport stopped spinning.

"We have to go over to the other side of the airport and pick up someone else," Mr. Minkowski said.

She hardly heard him, becoming numb. Joan walked between them, each holding one of her arms as they walked her out to their car. Her legs heavy, each step was difficult.

They drove to the side of the airport where the private jets landed. A small jet was just parking on the apron in front of the Aviation Services building. Mr. Minkowski left the car and walked over to the plane. The clam shell door opened and Meyer ambled out.

He talked to his dad for a moment and glanced at the car.

Joan slid out of the car, ran over to Meyer, and wrapped her arms around his neck. He put both of his arms around her and held her tightly as she began sobbing again.

As Meyer sat in the car Joan held him as tight as she possibly could. She thought that if she could just hold him tight enough, then she would be able to dissipate the overwhelming pain.

"Your grandmother Esther is at the hospital with your sister, Joan. We'll go there so you can be with them," Mr. Minkowski said. "I've rented a furnished apartment about a block from the hospital so Esther can be nearby."

Joan didn't respond, but rested her head on Meyer's shoulder. She whimpered quietly all the way.

As the car stopped in front of the hospital, Joan opened her door and started to get out. She looked back at Meyer. "Please come with me. I don't think I have the strength to do this alone."

Mr. Minkowski told Meyer, "I'll arrange for a rental car to be delivered to the hospital. If you need anything else call your mom or me."

"Thanks, Dad. I'll call you later with any updates."

As they walked into the hospital, Joan was holding Meyer's hand with both her hands. She was angry with God for doing this to her family, but thanked him for sending Meyer when she needed him so desperately.

Meyer inquired at the front desk for directions to Golda's room. They arrived on the proper floor and Joan saw her grandmother talking to a doctor. As soon as they looked at each other, they both started sobbing. Grandmother Esther gave her a huge hug.

"Are you ready for this?" the doctor asked.

Joan nodded.

Meyer put one arm around her and the other around her grandmother's shoulder.

"Your sister is still in critical condition but at least she can breathe on her own. She suffered quite a bit of facial trauma and you may not recognize her. Her pelvis is broken in three places. If she hadn't been wearing a seatbelt, she wouldn't have made it to the hospital. We have her heavily sedated and will keep her sedated until later tomorrow. It wouldn't hurt to talk to her even though she won't reply."

As they entered her room, Joan saw Golda was in an oxygen tent. She was covered with tubes, wires, and bandages. She walked in ahead of Meyer but as soon as she saw her sister's face she turned back to Meyer and buried her face in his chest.

Her body shook as she sobbed and kept asking, "Why? Why?"

Golda had purplish blotches over the non-bandaged parts of her face and arms. Her bruised eyelids were jammed shut from swelling. Her cheek and the left side of her jaw were purple and the jaw had a row of angry-looking stitches running down it. Her fiancé, Aaron, sat at her side holding her hand. He stood up and hugged Joan and shook Meyer's hand.

Grandma and Meyer each put an arm around Joan. Her sister's injuries were horrifying to look at. The doctor was correct. Golda was not recognizable.

Meyer and Aaron engaged in conversation.

Joan and her Grandma went out to the hallway.

"I have a huge favor to ask you, Grandma. I want to stay with you tonight because the rented apartment is near the hospital. I want Meyer to stay as well."

"That's fine, Joan."

"There's another favor, Grandma, but it's difficult for me to ask you this."

"I know, honey. You want to sleep with him tonight so he can hold you."

Joan's jaw dropped.

"Don't look at me with such surprise on your pretty face. When your grandfather, Manny, was alive it meant the world to me when he held me. I see the way Meyer looks at you, and I especially see how you look at him. Believe me, Joan. I would give anything to have Manny here with us tonight so he could hold me."

"Grandma, I should have known you'd understand." Joan wrapped her arms around her grandmother.

Around midnight, the three of them went to the apartment. Meyer and Joan slept on a foldout couch in the living room. Joan tried to sleep, but was getting overwhelmed by knowing she would never see her parents again. She had just started to get sleepy when she realized she would have to plan a funeral...life seemed to be giving her an emotional battering.

Meyer's parents assisted with her parents' funeral.

"God bless you for all you've done for us," she told them. "There were many times during the funeral, when the only reason I remained standing was that Meyer was holding me.

After the funeral, Meyer flew back to school and Joan moved into her parents' house.

Soon, they began to hear better news from the doctors. Golda was improving every few days. Three weeks later, as Joan and her Grandma walked down the hall toward her sister's room, she saw Golda's fiancé, Aaron, talking to the doctor. The doctor was smiling and Aaron had tears in his eyes.

"You have one tough sister," Aaron told her. "She woke up this morning and asked for something to eat."

"Does she know about our parents?"

The doctor replied, "She's still groggy from all the pain medication and she hasn't asked about them yet. You need to be prepared to tell her what happened to them. Her prognosis is much better than it was when you first arrived here. If this keeps up she'll have a chance at a fairly complete recovery. Be aware though, she's going to need lots of help for the next six months, minimum."

"Help we can give her. Thank God she's getting better," Grandma Esther said.

They all walked into the room. The oxygen tent had been removed and her sister looked at them and smiled briefly.

"Joan...Grandma..." Her voice trailed off. "If you're all here then—Aaron, what's going on? How are my parents?"

Aaron grasped her hand. "They didn't make it. I'm sorry."

"No. Please, no. Joan, please tell me it's not true—Grandma? It's not true."

"It's true Golda. They're gone." Quiet sobs filled the room.

• • • •

NO MATTER THAT SHE knew it was true, Joan couldn't believe she and Golda had lost their parents. It was surreal. When *Shiva* started she exchanged pleasantries with the people who came for the visitation, but otherwise had no interest in taking part in discussions of what everyone remembered about her parents. When she thought of them, Joan felt an anchor was dragging her emotions down. Whatever managed to keep her happy before the tragedy was no longer buoyed her spirit. She wanted to sleep all the time and experienced an unusual number of headaches. The endless greenery of the Northwest previously made her happy, but now her surroundings just felt gray and lonely. Her world was becoming a shell of what it once was. The rare times she went shopping for clothing the only colors that appealed were gray and black.

She was unable to put her emotional life back together. To avoid feeling any more pain, she created an emotional bubble of numbness. The battering she endured from her the loss of her parents, dragged Joan into depression.

With their parents gone, she and Golda felt cut off from family. They were very grateful that Grandma Esther was still around.

• • • •

GOLDA HAD A LONG TALK with Aaron before she left the hospital, telling him she might not be able to have children because her hips were so severely injured.

He grabbed her hands and kissed her cheek. "If you can't get pregnant we'll adopt. Don't worry about it now. We'll just concentrate on your recovery so we can be married."

When they were alone, Golda said to Joan, "I don't know why all this happened to us but I intend to spend the rest of my life giving back to Aaron the blessed kindness and support he's provided me during this ordeal."

On one of Joan's visits, one of the nurses spoke to Golda about Aaron. "He was talking to you the whole time you were unconscious. Some of the nurses were betting the first words you would say to him were going to be, 'Aaron, please stop talking.'"

He managed to see her every day after work and visited longer every weekend.

When the psychologist came by to see how Golda's emotional state was, she told him thanks for stopping by, but "I have my own psychologist and support system named Aaron. He is keeping my spirits up on a daily basis."

Joan and Grandma took turns visiting Golda at the hospital during the week days. They also had been getting her parents' home ready for Golda's arrival. Joan discovered Grandma Esther and Mr. Minkowski paid for modifications to make the house wheelchair accessible.

After eight weeks in the hospital, Golda finally came home with her beloved Aaron constantly at her side.

Joan's parents left her enough money to finish college and she arranged to take classes locally so she could stay in her parents' house that now belonged to her and Golda. Her life was settling into a routine of classes, taking care of Golda, and working a part time job.

She decided not to continue her relationship with Meyer. The thought of having a partner in her life who might depend on her, was more than her current emotional state could endure. He sent her some thoughtful letters; she replied as briefly as possible, her letters not really saying anything.

Eventually he took the hint and quit writing, which only added to her sense of sadness, feeling as if she'd betrayed him. They'd experienced so many great times during their childhood but she thought they had no future together. As depressed as she was, she felt he was better off with someone else.

Grandma Esther returned to the Midwest once Golda came home. On the weekends, Golda tried to get Joan to go out when Aaron was there to take care of her. She meant well, but Joan really preferred just staying around the house and sleeping or reading.

• • • •

THE YEARS PASSED BY as a gray blur for Joan. Golda and Aaron married and have been happily so for four years; and much to their delight, a child was on the way. Other than a slight limp you couldn't tell Golda had been in a terrible accident.

Joan was convinced that people could tell which house was theirs when they drove down their street—it was the one with the glow coming from Golda and Aaron's love and devotion to each other. She often thought they were the definition of a perfect couple.

When Joan's college degree was complete, she started doing tax accounting for some small businesses. She managed a brief relationship with one of the guys from school.

His name was Sam Stein. After they'd gone out a few times, her body was letting her know she needed to have sex with someone. She and Sam did it a number of times before he was shipped to Vietnam. There was no romance or emotion...it just relieved an urge. It certainly wasn't what she and Meyer shared. When Sam left for Vietnam they decided their relationship had no future. Joan let him know, he deserved someone who wasn't depressed all the time.

Within weeks of Sam's arriving in Vietnam, Joan received two life changing phone calls. The first call was from her gynecologist telling her she was pregnant. A week later, she received a call from Sam's parents asking her if she would attend his funeral as he had been killed in Vietnam.

As if she wasn't suffering enough mental anguish over her parents' death, now she had to decide if she wanted to keep the baby she and Sam created. She'd made up her mind to have an abortion when she learned about his death. Joan felt a responsibility to this man who had given his life for his country. He would never have a chance to have another child. Sam's parents would never have a chance at grandchildren as he had no siblings.

What impact would it have on this child if she brought it into the world without a dad? Would she be able to make a decent living for them? If she married someday, would her husband treat Sam's baby as his own? Joan was confused, with no clear direction and certainly no clear answers. The questions swirled in her mind in the way clothing twists and turns on a clothes line during a windy day.

She would have given anything to have the nerve to call Meyer to discuss all of this. Joan was quite sure she shouldn't interrupt his life...especially after being so mean to him concerning the way she ended their relationship. Certainly, she was the last person he wanted to hear from.

After more sleepless nights than she could count, Joan finally decided to keep the baby. A few months later she found out she was going to have a girl. She decided to name her Samantha, after her dad.

Joan drove out to view Mt. Rainer. The base and bottom two-thirds of the mountain were clear as a bell but the top one-third was obscured by clouds.

"That's the way my life looks. My future is certainly obscured just like the top of Rainier."

That day was the first time she felt Samantha moving inside her.

"We have to make some changes, Samantha. We're going shopping for colorful clothes. I'll do my best to make sure you enter a happy world with a together mom."

She started an exercise program for pregnant moms, which helped to a huge degree. Joan was sweating away her negative feelings and moodiness plus making new friends. Even Golda and Aaron told her she was noticeably happier.

Samantha's birth brought more joy into her life than she felt she deserved. During the day, while she was busy taking care of Samantha and running her tax accounting business from her townhome, she didn't have much time to worry about their life.

At night, however, she was concerned about their situation. Getting a decent night's sleep became a problem. She still worried about Samantha growing up fatherless. Her financial situation was on thin ice; any change would be problematic. Joan's doctor prescribed a sleeping aid which she depended on every night.

As Samantha passed her third birthday, she started asking why other kids had fathers and she didn't. Joan did her best to explain her father's death in a war, but her answers never satisfied her daughter.

Joan's social life was non-existent. As soon as a potential date found out she had a child, he would immediately lose interest. She dreaded the thought of raising Samantha by herself. She didn't know it then, but the Lord was watching her. In the years to come, just when she started thinking her physical and emotional state couldn't get any worse, He found a way to bring Meyer back into her life when she truly needed him the most.

Chapter Four ~ College, Larry and the Twins

MY MOM, AN INCREDIBLY wise mother, sent me to college near Ft. Lauderdale, Florida. "Meyer," she told me many years later, "I figured the sight of all those bikini-clad bodies at the beach would give you motivation to get good enough grades to stay and finish college."

She had a point—soon after arriving, I learned there was a school for airline stewardesses not far from our school. They were gorgeous, and they completed their training in eight weeks, which meant new trainees would arrive. Oh yeah, I had all the motivation I could handle.

Dad and Mom decided to sell the house I grew up in. They were going to move to a smaller home closer to Seattle. Briefly, I was sad to think I wouldn't ever go home to the same house again. It was, however, just a house. A home is the physical location where all the hearts gather.

I was still sad about my parting with Joan after our week at the cabin. I thought meeting and making new friends would compensate for the feeling of emptiness I felt at our parting, so I made a habit of trying to meet the quieter people in my classes.

One quiet classmate was a Business Management major who worked in a boatyard installing engines in Fiberglas boats—a fellow drummer, Larry Shapiro had a serious side when it came to studies, but he exhibited a quiet confidence when we went out in search of the not-so-elusive female.

Both our dads had insisted we get some kind of job while we were in school, and like me, Larry planned to stay in Florida and take classes over the summer to graduate as soon as possible.

"Hey Meyer, I get paid a hundred and fifty dollars for every engine I install at the boatyard. It takes from eight to twelve hours to install and test it. Would you like to help me? I'd split the fee fifty-fifty."

"Sounds great," I told him, even though I knew from my experience working with friends during high school, engine installation was a back breaking, knuckle busting kind of work. It would be especially miserable in the hot Florida sunshine.

We went out looking for an apartment to rent and found a small, two-bedroom unit not too far from the intra-coastal canal. It was walking distance to college and close to the boatyard where Larry worked. Since we could walk to school, I didn't need a car, but I wanted one for dating, so I called my dad to ask for car money.

"A car's a great idea," he told me. "I'll send you five hundred dollars and you get a job to pay me back. Also, be sure to save some of the money you earn for paying for your own books next semester."

*Well, since you put it that way, Dad...*so I looked for a decent job all that week, but found nothing. With classes starting the following week, I was getting desperate when Larry said he had four engines to install the next weekend and could use my help.

It would take the two of us all weekend to get them installed and tested. As the temperature was in the upper nineties and the humidity was tropical, I didn't look forward to the weekend's work. Three hundred dollars, however, would go a long way to paying back my dad.

The work was miserable, as I had anticipated. Fiberglas finishes was crude in those days, and if you weren't careful could cause days of itching.

I learned Larry's father was a cab driver in New York. Larry was the first person in their family to go to college, literally working his way through. He was becoming a friend and there was no way I could say no to him when he needed help. I became a regular part of the engine install team. While it continued to be miserable work, it was good money, and after a few weeks seeing what a hard worker he was, I found I too was adjusting to the work. I can honestly say our working together made us friends for life.

Shortly after second semester began, I received a call from my dad. He'd told me Joan's parents and sister had been in a terrible accident. Her dad had died at the scene, her mom died in surgery, and her sister wasn't expected to live the night. Dad set up a flight for me to come home right away.

It was a terrible few days. Joan seemed emotionally drained and more distant every day. I flew home after the funeral, but wrote a few letters her in the weeks after. She only answered with "how's the weather" kinds of responses, never really saying much. After all our great times growing up together, it seemed our relationship had hit a dead end. I buried myself in my studies and going out picking up girls. I didn't want to think about the painful emptiness I felt knowing Joan wouldn't be part of my life and—knowing that I couldn't protect her from everything after all.

I had a lot of friends at school and I'd met a number of girls from around the country who had come down to vacation in Ft. Lauderdale during spring break.

One sad episode occurred to my Jewish friend, Joseph Albert, during the spring break of our freshman year. We were on the beach and a drop-dead gorgeous girl stepped out of an open beer garden along the ocean front, wearing a blue bikini, big sunglasses, and flip flops on her feet. Her blonde hair cascaded out from under the tan, wide-brimmed, straw sunhat she was wearing. She was slim and likely six feet tall. If memory serves, at least five feet of those were legs.

"Hi, Tom," she called out to him.

"I'm Joseph, but if you would rather call me Tom, it's okay with me."

"Joseph—I am so sorry," she said to him in a beautiful southern drawl. "I didn't mean to forget your name."

"It's okay," he told her. "I've also forgotten your name."

"Well, honey, I'm Jeanette, and I'm from Atlanta, Georgia." She pronounced it *Alana*, instead of Atlanta. They had a great few days together. Besides being pretty, she was bright and had a great sense of humor.

As he related it to me, one morning, as Joseph was leaving to head off to his classes, he'd told her, "I'm having a great time with you. I hope you feel the same way."

"Ah do feel the same way, honey," she drawled. "Besides *ah'm* easy to please. The only thing I hate is Nigras and Jews." Let me tell you, Joseph did a perfect impression of her when he told me.

Joseph said he was so shocked that he fell silent for a moment, but then told her, "Well you should know, for the last couple of days you've been screwed by a high-yellow Jew."

Apparently, with a look of utter disgust on her face, she violently slammed the door of her hotel room as he left.

• • • •

OUR APARTMENT BUILDING was too noisy in the evenings so Larry and I started studying at the public library. We were sitting at a table with room for four, when I heard a young female voice say, "Can we sit with you guys?"

I looked up to see identical twin sisters smiling at us. Larry nodded in the affirmative, so I said sure.

Danielle and Michelle Warshawsky were sophomores in high school, serious about their studies, and drop-dead gorgeous. Cute, petite, and both wearing *Chai*'s on gold chains around their necks. Michelle was working on an AP biology project and Danielle was looking up information on ethics. It wasn't long before boys started stopping by our table to try to talk to the twins. One angry look from Larry or me and they would quickly leave.

As the library was about to close, Michelle whispered to Danielle, "I told you." Danielle grinned and Michelle said, "I thought the boys would leave us alone if we sat with you guys."

"And it worked," Danielle announced. "Thank you. I hope you don't mind but we told everyone you're our big brothers. Now no one will come over and bother us while we're studying."

Great, I always knew I would be useful for something one day.

The twins sat with us once a week for the next couple of months. Sometimes I helped Michelle with her AP bio and Larry would help Danielle research various ethics topics, occasionally sitting together in the lobby of the library discussing them. Larry seemed to love what I would call a big-brother role with Danielle.

After a few months, our apartment building settled down and we went back to studying there. We didn't see the twins again until we were invited to the local Synagogue for the first-night *Seder*, the special prayers and ritual meal on the first and second nights of Passover.

The twins were excited to see us and brought their parents over to meet us. We talked to them for a while before the *Seder* started and once their parents learned we were students from out of town; their mom invited us over to their house for second night *Seder*.

Larry and I would certainly accept an offer for a home cooked meal any time—but a home cooked *Seder* was to die for. We quickly agreed and they invited us to sit with them during the first night's *Seder*. It didn't seem significant at the time, but as Michelle and the twins' parents led Larry and me to the dinner table, Danielle pushed her way in front of me so she would be sitting next to Larry.

The *Seder* at the twins' house the following night was wonderful. Their parents were kind people who truly felt honored to have the chance to open their home to guests. We learned their father owned a business that made plastic pellets for extruding and molding. He told us Danielle was curious about the whys behind right and wrong from a young age. Michelle had to know how things worked. She especially wanted to learn the science behind diseases.

"My daughters look identical but they each think differently," he told us.

It was completely obvious the girls were the light of their parents' lives. Their mom told us, with obvious pride, which parts of the dinner her daughters had prepared.

• • • •

THE FOLLOWING SUMMER the Warshawsky family traveled to Israel. Before they left, Larry and I went over to their home and we each gave Danielle and Michelle eighteen dollars to donate as *Tzedakah* while they were in Israel. They could use the money for charity all in one location or divide it up. Upon their return they had to tell us how they distributed the money. This custom was to ensure a safe return. They loved the idea and promised to keep track of their donations.

During their trip Danielle wrote a lovely letter to Larry detailing what a wonderful time she and her family were having exploring Israel. At the end of the letter she posed an interesting ethics question. He replied with a four-page letter on possible solutions.

In her next letter to him, she suggested they both read a certain book on Jewish ethics they might discuss sometime in the future. Larry found it at the library and devoured it

"I'm an only child so having a little sister is special for me," he said.

I received a postcard from Israel with a picture of a restaurant in Tel Aviv on the front and on the back was the message, "We ate here—Michelle."

On the family's return we were invited for *Sabbath* dinner. They were excited about all they learned during their trip and could hardly wait to tell us.

Mr. Warshawsky told us with enthusiasm in his voice, "Everyone knows you can't grow corn in a desert—but the Israeli's are growing corn in the desert. Everyone knows you can't grow wheat in a desert—but the Israeli's are growing wheat in the desert."

He went on and on, telling us how the Israelis were making the desert bloom. Then, Larry, Danielle, and the twins' mom and dad, started discussing ethics while Michelle and I discussed the mathematics of chemistry and physics and what she could look forward to when she started studying calculus. At some point Danielle commented she wanted to visit our apartment.

"Not until you're eighteen," I said in an older brother sounding voice and everyone laughed.

I had classes early every morning that lasted until the mid-afternoon or later. My longest days were Mondays, Wednesdays, and Thursdays, but lucky Larry had no classes on Mondays or Wednesdays.

I learned some years later that the first Monday after Passover began the following spring, Danielle arrived at our apartment with a box of Matzo. Larry met her at the door and accepted the gift. As it happened, the twins' school was on spring break.

"Can I see your apartment?" she asked.

"Meyer and I agreed no one under eighteen is allowed inside. I know he's not here, but ethically speaking..."

He told me she gave him a huge smile and said, "I know. I know. You're still my big brother. Well big brother, how about going for a walk?"

So, off they went to the beach...then to a nature center...then to a hamburger joint for lunch. Larry said to me, it amazed him they never ran out of things to talk about—not that day or when they were together again on Wednesday and Thursday.

Michelle spent the next summer working and writing a research paper on some aspects of muscular dystrophy. She called me in tears one day and told me the paper she was trying to write was a disaster and could I please come to her home and look it over.

I arrived at the Warshawsky home and found their dining room table covered with papers and books. As I read Michelle's paper, I found it was horribly disorganized. I'd asked to see her outline and she showed me a couple of pages from a legal pad that probably should have been better used to wrap fish, rather than be the backbone of a research paper.

It took us four hours to rework the outline into a decent framework. I showed her where her ideas weren't explained clearly enough and where she needed more information to back them up.

"My college ID will get us into the tech libraries at the U in Miami, so we should head down there a couple of afternoons this week."

When we arrived at the library, I started filling out eight-by-five cards with sources from the Periodic Literature that Michelle might want to examine while she looked for books on the weak areas of her paper.

We repeated this activity four more times over the next few weeks and after many more weeks of hard work, she finally created, what I thought, what was an excellent bit of research. She submitted it for peer review. The peer review committee asked for some clarifications and a couple of changes. It was then published in a biological research journal.

Michelle called me and asked me to come over so she could give me a copy of the journal with her paper in it. She was absolutely beaming as she handed it to me. As I started examining her work, I saw she'd listed me as Assistant Researcher.

"You shouldn't have put me on there. This is *your* paper."

"You always took time to help me. Who turned my "only for fish wrapping" outline into the backbone of the paper? If my writing wasn't clear, you helped me clarify my thoughts. I never would have had the time to find all the information and sources without your help. You were the library expert. You patiently taught me all the organic chemistry I needed to understand. In the four months it took me to write this paper, you never once told me you were too busy to help."

If I was the library expert, it was due to a small-town librarian in the Northwest who taught Joan and me how to look up things when we were young. God bless that librarian, wherever she is.

"Well—thank you for including me, but that's what big brothers are for."

Michelle embraced me. "Thank you, big brother."

• • • •

THE FOLLOWING FALL, a fifty-foot Chris Craft Constellation limped into the boatyard. It needed both engines and transmissions replaced. The new owner also hired a carpenter to repair a lot of the woodwork. The once proud boat was the equivalent of a nautical bag lady, but with new Ford engines replacing her original Lincoln engines, new transmissions, and repaired woodwork, she would once again look and sound like the dignified lady she was intended to be.

Larry loved working on the boat and often asked the carpenter questions on how he repaired the beautiful wood joinery. The boatyard hired one of our friends, who worked on leather car interiors, to repair the furniture in the cabin of the Connie.

As I helped install the engines and was better at boat handling, I drove the Connie onto the Atlantic for a test run. The rebuilt boat demonstrated her designed-in stability and ease of handling. She was a safe, stable, and dignified cruiser needing only minimal tuning to perfect her. The newer electronics we added worked well and complimented her already capable cruising abilities. When we tied her to the dock, we learned the owner had been arrested for counterfeiting.

Within days, the boatyard put a mechanics' lien on the boat and immediately put it up for sale hoping to get some of their money back. Fiberglass boats were beginning to be all the rage, but the Connie was mahogany and teak—beautiful mahogany and teak, mind you. Unfortunately, the wood took a lot more maintenance than fiberglass, but looked immaculate if you put in the time to properly care for it. The Connie wasn't being sold at a fire-sale price, but it was pretty low.

Before the paint dried on the for-sale signs, Larry convinced his father to front him the down payment money and he purchased the boat. He was so excited—like a little kid with a new toy. He rented covered dock space at the boatyard where we worked so we could keep an eye on her, and then spent nearly every spare moment working on the old girl. Larry kept it so clean, I was certain dust wouldn't dare settle on it. The Connie was named Salty Boot and I kept asking him if he was going to rename it.

With a Cheshire-cat grin on his face, all he would say is, "I've plans."

The following spring Larry and I decided we should take the Connie on a four-day trip down to the Keys during our college spring break. Lots of students from around the country would be there and it would be a great time. It would be especially great traveling on our own boat.

· · · ·

MICHELLE AND DANIELLE celebrated their eighteenth birthday on a Tuesday evening. Mrs. Warshawsky had put together a lovely birthday dinner for the twins. Many of their friends were invited, including Larry and me, but I was finishing a paper for school so I didn't make it. Larry did attend and told me Mr. Warshawsky was spending more and more time talking business with him. Larry told him we were planning to take the Connie down to the Keys the following weekend.

It was early Friday morning, when I heard two people knocking on our front door and giggling something terrible. I opened the door and found the twins standing there grinning at me. They were wearing matching white short-sleeve blouses and denim short-shorts. Each had a florescent bikini top on under their blouse.

"Well, aren't you going to invite us in?" Danielle was grinning ear to ear.

"Let me guess, you've turned eighteen."

They collapsed in peals of delighted laughter.

"Where's Larry?" Danielle asked.

"He's probably still asleep. He's a much sounder sleeper than I am. I'll tell him we have visitors."

Danielle pushed me aside. "No you won't. I will."

"He might not be decent."

She turned to me then, and if looks could talk, hers was saying, she had plans and I better not interfere. Danielle quietly opened the door to Larry's room, went in, and loudly slammed the door shut.

Larry yelled, "What the hell!" This was followed by laughter, as if two little kids were tickling each other, and then, of course, silence.

I turned to Michelle. "Something I should know?"

She told me how Danielle said she was going to marry him after the first night she and Larry discussed ethics. "At the time, I told my sister, he's just a boat engine installer and didn't she have higher aspirations for herself—we didn't know anything about you guys except you were students and installed boat engines. I remember her telling me, 'He's in school so I'm sure he'll be able to take care of a family, but I'll tell you the truth, when he smiles at me, I know I wouldn't care if he was a camel jockey.' For months afterward we kept referring to Larry as the camel jockey."

We both laughed.

"They've been going out for long walks the last couple of months, you know. I ran interference for Danielle at the birthday dinner and made sure Larry was seated next to her. At one point, I noticed Larry put his hand on Danielle's arm to get her attention then, as if her hand had a mind of its own, she grabbed his and they sat there holding hands under the table, talking with people, looking as if nothing special was going on.

Finally, Danielle looked as if she might burst and she leaned over, whispered something to him and they left the table. She told me earlier that day that she was finally telling Larry how she felt about him. They snuck upstairs. She told me everything that happened, although I would have known anyway—we are twins you know! Do you want me to tell you?"

I nodded.

"Well, she told me they entered her room, she closed the door, and still facing away from—because she was afraid of his reaction—she said, 'Larry, I have something difficult to tell you.' Then, in one motion he spun her around, and kissed her. Happy as a clam, she said she slid her arms around his neck and they kissed for a long time—I guess he felt the same about her all this time too. Danielle said she felt herself warming from the kiss and embrace, but she felt joyfully secure with his arms around her."

I understood that feeling—I remembered when he'd first felt it with Joan.

"Danielle told me she was certain Larry felt the same way about her and she never wanted him to let go. She said he grinned at her and said, 'Happy eighteenth birthday, special lady.' And she asked him, 'I'm not your little sister anymore?' To which he replied, that he knew from early on how special she was and he knew they would end up together. He said, 'Danielle Warshawsky, I don't know what the future holds, but I know for certain I want my future to include you.' To which, Danielle told me, she kissed him again and again."

I wondered why Larry hadn't said anything about this. Perhaps he was unsure of how she felt about him, too.

"Remember the first night when Danielle asked Larry to walk with her to the lobby of the library and they talked about ethics?"

"Certainly. You and I had chatted about our mutual interests as well."

"Well, Danielle made some notes on what they'd talked about and when she looked them over later, she wrote the word *Bashert* on the same notebook page. She saved the page and showed it to him when they were in her room. They talked about how she'd felt sometimes when she acted childish and became angry over silly things, but Larry never became angry with her. He'd always stayed calm and talked to her until she calmed down."

Michelle had a sympathetic look on her face, thinking of her twin sister. "Afterwards, she always felt terrible about her behavior. A few times she even came home crying because she thought she acted so horribly, he wouldn't want to spend time with her. But that never happened and they managed to spend more and more time together. When I saw the way he smiled at her, I knew he thought of Danielle as a special person."

"I guess I was too busy to notice."

"Danielle felt that there were plenty of times in the last two years he could have taken advantage of her—and she would have let him, believe me—but he never did. She told Larry she knew in her heart she wanted to spend the rest of her life paying him back for waiting for her to grow up. She said she wanted to make a home for them so filled with joy and laughter, everyone would be jealous of their relationship."

"I had no idea."

"Larry told her it wasn't easy for him to wait either but he was afraid if he did take advantage of her, it might destroy their relationship, and there was no way he was going to let that happen. He told her to start shopping for a formal dress because she was going to be his date to our school's formal dance next month. She said that she tried to tell him how much she loved him then, but she couldn't because she was crying."

That made Michelle happy as well. Her eyes filled with tears as she related the story.

"She told Mom and Dad that you and Larry were going down to the Keys later in the week. Larry said we should join you. And surprisingly, my folks thought it was okay. Later I heard Dad said to Mom, 'After all these years taking such good care of the twins, they aren't going to do anything to hurt them. In fact, the twins are going to come home filled with a million stories of what fun they had.' So, those two have spent the last two days shopping for this trip."

"Outrageous."

"There are two coolers in our car with everything needed for four people to sustain themselves on a four-day boat trip."

"Larry and your sister are magic. I thought they were close but only brother-sister close."

"Meyer—you watch and see. Danielle won't let Larry get more than an arm's length away from her."

Her expression changed. "We have to try something, Mr. Minkowski." Michelle stood in front of me and, standing on her tiptoes, gave me a long kiss.

She stepped back. "Well?" she asked. "What do you think?"

I replied, "Honestly, it was as if I was kissing my sister. How was it for you?"

"I've never kissed my sister that way, but if I ever do, I suspect it will feel the same. You and I are headed in different directions, aren't we?"

• • • •

IT WAS A SUNNY DAY with an incredible blue, nearly-cloudless sky. As we walked up the pier toward the now-gleaming Connie, resplendent in her new woodwork, I noticed the name of the boat had finally been changed. It read *Danielle's Dory*.

Danielle shouted, "Larry, you named your boat for me!"

"Not quite," he replied with a grin. "I renamed *our* boat for you." Kissing ensued between them until I was wondering if they were going to board the boat or just stand there and kiss.

Michelle was right. They were never more than an arm's length away from each other the entire voyage and were magic for each other. They argued about ethics and laughed and joked and giggled constantly. They teased and played tricks on each other. *Danielle's Dory* began filling with laughter and joy. I am sure the old mahogany and teak still rings with the joy and laughter those two created.

We loaded the boat with our supplies and prepared to get under way. Then we men reviewed some of the safety rules with the girls, but the young ladies were so excited it's doubtful they listened. Larry pulled in the docking lines and I brought the Connie's deep throated engines rumbling to life.

Meyer was at the helm because he was more adept a boat handling. Larry and Danielle cared little for who was at the helm because they were already making a place to lay next to each other on the Connie's broad bow. They had so many cushions, towels, and blankets piled up there, it almost looked like a nest.

Churning into the Atlantic, the air cooled so Michelle and I put on sweatshirts. Larry and Danielle wrapped themselves in blankets and used body heat to keep each other warm. Danielle brought along a stack of books, each had pieces of paper bookmarking where she would find ethics questions they could discuss.

Michelle assisted at the helm. In between navigation duties and watching out for other boaters, we reviewed material for her AP

Chemistry final. The Connie cruised a sedate sixteen knots, the Atlantic was calm, and the ride was smooth and easy down to the Keys. We docked as close as we could to the John Pennekamp Coral Reef State Park.

The next day our foursome went on a glass-bottomed boat tour to see the coral and the other magnificent sea creatures living there. The following day we rented a shallow draft boat which we used to get out next to the stunning reefs, then carefully dropped anchor so as to not damage the beautiful coral heads.

With mask, snorkel, and fins, we swam over the amazing corals waving in the current. Some of the smaller fish were so curious they would swim up to our masks as if trying to peer into the swimmer's eyes.

After dinner, I sat on the screen-enclosed rear deck of the Connie reviewing some math proofs I would be presenting after the trip. I stopped my review, poured myself a glass of wine, then thought of the immense beauty seen at the Pennekamp State Park. From below deck, Danielle and Larry started laughing.

I suddenly felt an overwhelming sadness that I couldn't share this nautical adventure with a girl I knew from the Northwest. Joan would have been fascinated by every creature. If she had seen the sea turtle which passed us, her joy would have endured for days. Michelle saw my sadness and asked if I was okay.

"Thinking of a friend I lost."

The following morning, Larry and I woke up early and set the table on the rear deck for breakfast. When everything was prepared, I called Michelle and said we needed to go for a short walk.

"Let's eat first. I'm starving."

In a stern voice I told her, "We're going for a walk—*now*."

"Okay, Okay. You don't have to be grouchy about it."

Larry called Danielle up on deck just after the we two left. After a few minutes, I heard Danielle's scream.

"What happened?"

"She found the ring. Larry just served her a flute of champagne with an engagement ring in the bottom of the glass. We can walk back to the boat now."

"You knew?"

"Not only did I know, but your mom and dad know as well."

Back on deck, the two sisters looked at each other, screamed, and shared a big hug.

Danielle showed the ring to Michelle. "Not bad for a camel jockey," she said.

Michelle and I laughed but poor Larry didn't understand the joke.

We all had a great time in the Keys, but for Michelle and me it was definitely the big-brother-little-sister kind.

It was obvious, to the entire world if they'd seen it, that Larry and Danielle were meant for each other. Larry went to work with the twins' dad after graduation. They moved into the apartment Larry and I shared during college while Danielle attended college nearby—Michelle attended a University in Boston. Danielle and Larry were married a year later and she went on to complete a PhD—in ethics, of course.

The last few weeks of my last year in college turned out to be quite depressing. I received a message from Uncle Sam. It started with the phrase, Greetings from your President—I had been drafted into the army.

Thoughts of Joan were now far from my mind. At the end of the year I went over to say good-bye to the twins and their parents.

The last thing Michelle told me was, "When I find Mr. Right, believe me he isn't going to be one of you math or science geeks. If I'm ever on a date with a guy who pulls out a slide rule, it will signify the sudden death of the date, and the relationship."

Life does turn out differently than expected as certainly would be the case for Michelle.

Mr. Warshawsky told me, "Please take care of yourself while you're in the army. Come back in one piece and look me up. I'll have a job for you."

Chapter Five ~ Vietnam

I WASN'T IN GOOD PHYSICAL condition when I reported for Basic Training—unless it was the kind of physical condition needed to drive to the bookstore to buy another book. In fact, prior to the army, when I got the feeling I should exercise, I usually laid down until the feeling passed.

Unfortunately, when I got to Fort Polk I had to wait two weeks for my Basic Training class to begin. We were kept busy doing lawn maintenance and painting chores, interspersed with some short hikes. I was getting bored out of my mind toward the end of the first week.

This taught me an important lesson—never let your complaints be overheard by a sergeant.

We had just received our uniforms and boots and a sergeant overheard me complaining about the boring work. He asked if I had been to college—yes I had—and if I would volunteer to help with a problem. Thinking anything was better than what I'd been doing, I enthusiastically replied in the affirmative.

"Follow me."

As we walked, he asked what my major was in college.

"Mathematics," I proudly replied.

"Perfect for this assignment and it may take a couple of days to complete."

We walked to an area next to the company headquarters building. There were eight of my fellow inductees standing there. The sergeant asked them to line up in a straight line.

"Okay, raise your left hand," he told them.

A flurry of left and right hands went up in the air. The hands started alternating as the men looked at each other, figuring the guy next to them probably knew which one was left.

"Okay, quit flapping your arms," the sergeant bellowed as he turned to me. "Okay, college man, can you see the problem?"

I could and figured that within an hour I would have it worked out. Two hours later, the sergeant came by and saw I made almost no progress. He gave me two dollars and told me to run to the PX and buy two lipsticks. Upon my return he took one of the lipsticks and wrote an L on the left hand of each of my students. He told them they couldn't wash it off until every one of them knew their left from right.

Wearing lipstick on their hands was an absolute nightmare for the men.

"If one of my friends from back home saw me with lipstick on my hand, I would die of shame—but not before my friends died of laughter"

A couple of hours later, the sergeant came by again and I could at least demonstrate some progress. If I lifted my right arm as I faced them and told them to lift their left arm, they mostly raised their left arm.

"Not bad." He turned to the men and shouted. "Okay, now listen up. Right Face!"

A few turned right and a few turned left, and at least two did a complete three-hundred-sixty turn.

The sergeant turned back to me. "Keep going, son."

"Yes, Sergeant."

Later in the evening, I noticed two of the men from my class were working hard at shining their boots until they looked like patent leather. I asked why.

"The army done give me my first pair of new shoes," one replied smiling.

"Hell, the army done give me the first set of new clothes I ever done had!" said the other one.

They were both from the mountains of Appalachia and they would become two of my best buddies in the army. By the end of the next day I could demonstrate to the sergeant all eight men knew their left hand from their right and could follow left and right face commands.

"Ready for Basic Training," he exclaimed.

The men thanked me for helping them and said if I ever needed help they would be right there to assist me—it was not just idle talk.

A month later, on a long hike, the heavy-set man walking next to me twisted his knee and fell. As I helped him get his rather substantial bulk on his feet again, I asked if I should request permission for him to ride in a Jeep. He said no, he wanted to finish with everyone else. I got under his left arm to try to take some of the weight off his strained knee. After about a hundred yards I was sweating profusely, when, without any prompting from me, my left-right buddies came up and took turns with me helping our fellow soldier complete the hike.

• • • •

A FEW WEEKS LATER, we were sleeping in tents and I was having a terrible time getting enough sleep. This led to another lesson; never open your mouth without thinking, even if you're going to tell the truth.

I was marching about halfway down, on the outer, right-hand side of a column of about one hundred men. We were been marching straight for the longest time when the column abruptly turned left. I kept going and tumbled into a ditch on the side of the road.

A sergeant came running over, and as I was getting to my feet he asked, "What happened to you?"

Unfortunately, I told him the truth. "I must have fallen asleep, Sergeant."

"What? You...you..." he stammered, "...you can't fall asleep when you're marching. Nobody falls asleep when they're marching. Don't tell me you fell asleep while you're marching! I know you're one of them college boys who think you know so much—every July we get you college clowns, and you don't even have enough sense to know you can't fall asleep when you're marching!"

His face was getting so red and he was so agitated, I thought he would have a heart attack right there. I sanitized the above quote, by the way, as in reality the sergeant repeatedly interjected comments during his rage at me. Apparently my family lineage was suspect, he was certain my brains—if I had any—were in my posterior area, and I was the dumbest four-letter-word-starting-with-F he ever encountered. All in all, quite an accomplishment, I'd say.

• • • •

A FEW MONTHS INTO BASIC Training we had our first inspection. Men who got excellent marks would get a twenty-four-hour pass to go into town. The guy I shared a bunk with and I stayed up all Friday night to make sure everything was perfect. We even went out and bought new toothbrushes to put in our lockers so we wouldn't have to worry about cleaning our old ones. We made up our bunks so tight you could bounce a quarter off them. We were ready.

As the sergeant came down the line, I heard him pointing out things other soldiers had performed incorrectly. I knew we had done those things correctly. When he got to my bunk, he was quiet for quite a while as looked over my gear. I remember thinking the pass was just a moment away. And then he picked up my new toothbrush.

"This is dirty," he told me with a huge grin on his face.

I couldn't believe it. He held up my new toothbrush and, sure enough, there was dust in the hole at the bottom of the toothbrush. My buddy and I got passes, but we were so tired from staying awake on Friday night, we just slept away our time off base.

During Basic Training in company Alpha Two-Two, we were taught the following company motto by our assistant drill instructor. We used it whenever we started a new training class during the first two weeks.

We are A-Two-Two, sir—We are happy to be training for the infantry.

A senior drill sergeant was assigned to us two weeks later. When he heard the company motto, he was furious.

"Soldiers don't talk that way," he spat at us.

Immediately, we got a new motto.

A-Two-Two—we are the Tigers. Big fucking Tigers with a dick this big! Whereupon we would hold up our hands, spread a yard apart.

I'll never be sure if the motto taught me how to talk as a soldier, but when one hundred and ten, nineteen to twenty-two–year-old men, shouted it out, we did get some laughs.

• • • •

THE SHOOTING RANGES were entertaining as I had many years of experience with pistols and rifles before I was drafted. On one of our first range exercises, I was doing awfully well and one of our drill sergeants asked if I would go down to the end of the line and help one of the guys. He was having a terrible time trying to hit anything.

"He seems to be doing just what I tell him, but he rarely hits the target," the sergeant told me. "See if you can tell what he's doing wrong while I work with some of the others."

I tried to work with the guy. No luck. He would hit the target about one out of every seven shots... I noticed he was squinting a lot. "Did you wear glasses when you were a civilian?

He replied emphatically, "Hell no. I ain't defective."

I asked him to read a nearby sign. It had four lines of twelve-inch-high block letters and was fifteen yards away.

"I can't read the sign 'cause them letters is moving too dang much."

Two days later he was one of the best shots on the range, courtesy of his new glasses. He did finally admit his eyes were defective, but insisted, in a rather loud and forceful manner to anyone who would listen, "Nothin' else about me is defective."

• • • •

DURING MY SECOND WEEK in Vietnam, we were taking a break from our seemingly never-ending hikes near a bridge over the Troi River. An old Vietnamese lady slowly walked past us. One of the Vietnamese children, who followed us everywhere when we were near villages, told me she was more than ninety.

She had a thoroughly wrinkled face. Her shoulders were bent forward and her spine was curved as if she had spent many years carrying heavy loads on her back. She held a walking stick in gnarled, arthritic hands and walked with a slow gait, as if each step was painful. I walked next to her for a few steps and asked her if she thought the Americans would make things better for the Vietnamese.

Her gaze shifted from straight in front of her to glance up at me. Without slowing her walk she smiled briefly at me. "A young Frenchman asked me the same thing twenty years ago."

• • • •

AT ONE POINT DURING my sojourn in Vietnam, our combat platoon was told to hike out of the jungle to a main road so trucks could pick us up to move us to a new location. We'd hiked like madmen, hacking our way through the thick jungle to get to the main road many miles from our starting point. It took three long, strength-sapping days to get there and we were absolutely exhausted by the time we arrived.

We radioed we were ready to be picked up and were told trucks would be there the next day. The next day we were told the trucks would be there the following day. After a week of this, a helicopter was sent out to bring us more food and water. All the second week, we were told the trucks would be there the next day.

An additional week and the trucks arrived.

We clambered aboard and were driven two miles down the road to our new location. Crazy.

The troops often had little to do during the daytime and sometimes we would walk down to the village open-air market to see what they had for sale. The villagers were often cooking different things and some of the fragrances weren't too pleasant. If fact, if the wind was coming at us from the direction of the market, we would just turn around and go back to our day position.

We were warned repeatedly not to eat things from the local market. One of the platoon mates violated the rule. About an hour later, he walked away from the day position as he felt a bout of diarrhea coming on. He dropped his pants and as soon as he squatted, he started vomiting as well.

A little Vietnamese boy, about eight years old, was standing next to me observing this awful sight. He grabbed my hand, the little one's eyes opened wide. He yelled in astonishment, "Look, man, he coming out his both ends!"

Ah, yes. We soldiers were a talented lot!

Another time, the platoon had been hiking through the humid jungle in one-hundred-plus-degree heat for a number of weeks and hadn't had a chance to wash. I mentioned to their lieutenant that we should find a place to clean up, as we smelled so bad even the mosquitoes weren't landing on us. We proceed to a twenty-foot-wide and one-foot deep stream.

After posting sentries, I decided to just lay down, fully clothed, in a small pool at the side of the stream. As I luxuriated in the cool water, I noticed the clear water cascading over my left sleeve was turning grey as it headed downstream. I dug a bar of soap out of my pack and soaping up my entire uniform while still wearing it, thinking it would be the best way to clean it. I rinsed the clothing and put them on boulders to dry. I had to wash my army-short hair a number of times to get all the sand and dirt off my scalp.

A few hours later, we were back to hiking and I thought I must have gotten good and clean as the cruel, unrelenting mosquitoes were landing on me again.

Then there was the day I earned the, thankfully temporary, nickname Mighty Monkey Shooter. We were hacking our way through some heavy jungle growth and cut a trail up to the top of a small rise to set up for the night.

I was pulling guard duty on the trail in the middle of the night and I sat with my legs folded and my M16 across my lap. There was lots of moonlight so I didn't think anyone could come up the trail without me easily spotting them. Halfway through my one-hour shift I heard a noise a few feet in front of me.

Oh, God, I thought, *someone got in front of me.*

I immediately rolled onto my side, expecting to see the flashes of my enemy's rifle firing at me, and I fired a burst from my M16 at the foe. The moonlight then revealed the terrified, and now screaming, face of a small monkey who noisily tore his way into the jungle. I didn't hit the monkey but my platoon mates teased me mercilessly the next few days.

This wasn't the only animal encounter. There was the time we had been ferried from our usual jungle area of operations to the highlands for a mission. We were in a large, open, grassy area and had stopped for a break, when suddenly some elephants were coming into view.

They were some distance away and not walking toward us, but would occasionally look in our direction and raise their trunks high into the air as if checking for our scent.

A guy from Kentucky, who loved hunting, whispered to us, "Don't shoot at 'em. These little M16 rounds will probably just piss 'em off."

We called in a few artillery shells to land in between us and the elephants and they hurriedly wandered away.

• • • •

ONE OF MY PLATOON MATES received a wound that opened up the top of his thigh in the same way a plow opens a furrow of dirt. I had run out of thread to close wounds, so I gathered safety pins—a trick I'd learned from reading a book about infantry soldiers in WWII. I lay across his stomach so he couldn't see what I was doing, and closed the wound with the safety pins. He cursed me mightily from all the pain I caused him. He didn't pass out, however, until I sat up and he saw the row of safety pins holding his thigh together.

Injuries I could handle, and I didn't fear being killed as much as the thought of being captured and then tortured to death. My fear of being killed had more to do with what my family would go through if that happened.

During my year in Vietnam my mother told me she watched in horror as a car with army markings slowly drove through our neighborhood, as if looking for an address. It was how relatives were informed their sons or daughters had been killed. The car drove on and wasn't seen again, but Mom related she was in such shock, she couldn't get anything done until she received a letter from me dated after the date the army car drove by.

Lucky for me, after six months in combat, the army discovered I could type, so I became a legal clerk. I was helicoptered out of the jungle to an office at the headquarters of the 101st Airborne Division. I transitioned from being a dirt-covered grunt to a legal clerk in a brigade HQ office where I received a clean uniform to wear every day, and best of all, I could shower every day.

The water for the showers was unheated, but after six months hiking around in the jungle and getting shot at occasionally, this was a huge improvement. Part of my office job was forwarding notices of those who were killed in action. I remember one July day in particular, as the day we received the notice one of my platoon mates had been killed.

Dan was a tall, gangly guy with an infectious smile. He was a friend to everyone in our platoon. When a new guy arrived he was the first person out to enthusiastically meet him and introduce him around. As I was a science kind of guy who also loved politics, Dan and I spent many a jungle hike debating those topics.

I felt a terrible emptiness knowing he was gone. I also felt angry because he deserved better.

It struck me, as I read the notice—there was a family in Ohio who didn't know their son was coming home in a box. But I knew. And the sorrow of what they were going to experience overwhelmed me. I didn't let my emotions show when I was in combat, but I could afford the luxury now, because I was a legal clerk in a secure area.

I briefly corresponded with a girl from New Jersey. After exchanging a few letters, she wrote how she spent a day decorating a gym for an upcoming dance. It wasn't fair of me, but I felt angry she spent an entire day making and placing decorations while my friends were still being shot at. I didn't write to her again.

My one year in Vietnam brought me in contact with some of the best men from across the states I have ever known. It gave me the belief if you ever see someone in uniform, or wearing some item indicating they were in the military, you should always take the time to shake their hand and thank them for serving. It's sad to think of how many soldiers come home and feel their service is not appreciated—none more than many of the Vietnam-era vets.

My Uncle Mike and I were not close until I came home from Vietnam. He was also a combat vet of the 101st but he was at Bastogne—"Battle of the Bulge"—among other WWII actions. One entire evening, he and I swapped war stories. It turns out I was the only person in the family he told about his war experience. He thought I was the only one who would understand the mental and physical challenges a fellow infantryman went through.

After I was discharged, I contacted some friends and started putting my life back together. Mr. Warshawsky, the twins' dad, was as good as his word. When I called him to tell him I was home safe and sound, he told me about a friend of his who worked in finance and wanted to open an office in Seattle. He knew my Math degree would be perfect for the job. I was hired, but also started work on a PhD in math as well.

I called Larry and was happy to hear he and Danielle were still as happy as can be. I told them I would be back to see them one day.

Chapter Six ~ Reunited

A NUMBER OF YEARS AFTER I came home from the army, I was at Oak Stream outdoor shopping their annual Labor Day weekend art show. There were many booths of artists using all kinds of media. I was quite particular about the art I purchased, but usually managed to find something I wanted to buy at this show.

While my mathematics career was proving to be a financial success, my personal life was pretty empty. By my current age of twenty-six, I had a number of relationships during and since college, but none of them continued for long. I started wondering if I was going to be a bachelor all my life.

As I walked around the show I stopped at a booth showing abstract as well as incredibly photo-realistic paintings of streams and forests. A four-year-old girl was proudly telling me her mother's paintings were displayed. She was quite petite with sparkling, bright, blue eyes, and a broad infectious smile that made you smile back. She pointed to one painting of a stream running through a forest.

"Can you see the minnows?" the little girl asked me.

"Yes, I see them. Did you know minnows are great for baking in pies?"

The little girl looked at me quizzically, as if trying to determine if I was serious. "No they're *not*." Then she laughed an amazingly melodic laugh, while her intense blue eyes sparkled.

I immediately knew who her mother was. I turned to look around the booth and there she was. It was Joan—with those amazing blue eyes and incredible warm smile. But she looked tired and worn—her shoulders seemed to droop and her skin was pale, similar to a physically and mentally exhausted soldier who had been in battle too long.

"Hey, you," she said with a big smile. "It's been a long time."

"Yes, a long time."

Hands on hips, the little version of Joan asked, "Mommy, do you know this guy?"

"Yes, Samantha. Actually I know every inch of him and he knows every inch of me." Joan laughed melodically, just as her daughter's had moments before.

We sat in two camp chairs at the back of the booth while four-year-old Samantha kept an eye out for customers.

"I've been to college and I've been to war. I was lucky—I came home healthy, both physically and mentally, unlike many of my Vietnam buddies."

"I didn't fight in the war," Joan said, "but the war fought with me. I was spending time with a friend from college named Sam, just before he went to Vietnam. A few weeks after he left, I discovered I was pregnant. I was considering an abortion when his parents called me and said he was coming home—..." Joan paused for a few seconds, lowered her voice so her daughter wouldn't hear. "You know, in a box. They asked if I would come to his funeral, as they knew we'd been friends." She shifted uncomfortably. "But that's all we were. I wasn't going to marry him. We weren't even going to write to each other while he was in Vietnam. But then, there I was, carrying his baby. How could I abort his only child? He would never have another chance—I was sleepless for weeks trying to decide what to do, but finally decided to have Sam's baby." She nodded to Samantha.

She went on to tell me of her art career. It brought her lots of joy and supplemented her minimal income as a tax accountant.

Samantha came over to let me know she made a painting as well, but her mom wouldn't let her sell it. I asked if I could see it and she raced to the back of the booth and opened a large plastic container labeled Samantha's Stuff. She returned with a notebook page sized canvas with lots of color and not much discernible shape.

"Do you see them?" she asked.

I took a guess. "Of course, I see those minnows."

"Mom, he sees them," Samantha screamed in delight.

Joan, again without smiling, said to Samantha, "Believe me, little lady, this guy knows about minnows."

I asked if I could buy the painting.

The four-year-old said, "Please, Mom, you sell..."

Before she could finish, a customer entered the booth. Joan approached the woman.

"Mom," Samantha yelled. "I was talking and you just walked away." She turned to Meyer. "That wasn't nice."

"Why don't we walk over to the bookstore and see if we can find a book for you?" he said.

"A book for me?"

"Come on." He held out his hand. She reached up and grabbed it.

As he left the booth, he yelled to Joan, "Bookstore."

She glanced at him with an unsure expression then turned back to her customer.

The four-year-old kept up a constant chatter about her friends, her bookshelf at home, and the activities she and her mom did together.

"I can't read yet," she said.

"Yes you can. You just need the right books."

We perused the children's section and I found a beginning reader with a picture for every word on the page. Samantha's reading habit began with *One Fish, Two Fish, Red Fish, Blue Fish* by Dr. Seuss. The little one was in heaven, bouncing up and down holding my hand the whole time we waited in line to pay for the book.

Arriving back at the booth, Joan was busy with a customer. Meyer sat on one of the camp chairs. Samantha came over, proudly holding her new book and told him her mom always reads to her, but now she can read, "So, I'm going to read my very own new book to you."

She cleared her throat. "Now remember, when you read a book you can always learn something," she told me in a Joan-like voice.

The little one climbed onto my lap and leaned back against me. We began working our way through the words and pictures. After the second time through, Samantha was yawning. She gave me the book, put her little head down on his chest, and fell sleep.

Okay. So picture it—there I was, this amazingly cool, twenty-six-year-old single guy who was suddenly stuck in an old friend's art display with a sleeping four-year-old lying against his chest. I would have died of embarrassment if one of my cool, single buddies came by and saw me. But barring that, to tell the truth, what I actually found to be amazing was how natural it felt to have Samantha's little body curled up against me.

Joan sat down next to us, and in between interruptions from customers we did our best to catch up. She told me how numerous guys had asked her out, but once they found out she had a child they were no longer interested. Then six months ago, she discovered she had breast cancer and underwent a mastectomy a month later.

She said the mental drain of feeling deformed and ugly was more difficult to endure than the physical pain of recovery from the surgery. Joan also endured a dreadful fear she would be raising Samantha alone.

"I was dating someone whose company I enjoyed," she said. "He was good with Samantha, and just when I thought we might have a future together, I found out about the cancer. Shortly after I told him I was going to have a mastectomy, he quit calling. I called him once and asked what was going on, but all he told me was, he was busy. What a jerk he turned out to be. Just when I so desperately needed someone, he abandoned me. I learned in my cancer recovery support group that breast cancer sometimes leads to divorce."

"Sad you had to go through so much crap."

"Part of some people's lives, I guess."

"You still with him?"

She shook her head. "Occasionally. The thought of starting a new relationship...would take too much time and energy. It's enough trying to keep up with a four-year-old. What about you?"

"Finished a PhD. in mathematics of finance, have my own consulting firm but no one in my life."

"Why not?"

"Being in combat...watching friends die...left scars on my soul which I suspect will never heal...makes it hard to spend time with someone who doesn't understand the pain. Without warning, I become depressed and feel like ripping someone's head off. I take it out on the nearest person."

"Not good."

"Before I worked as a consultant, my fellow employees tried to avoid working with me as they didn't know when the volcano would explode...sometimes little things...and I would lose it."

"Not the sweet Meyer I once knew."

"Not even close."

We didn't talk for a few minutes until Joan looked at Samantha sleeping on my lap. "Samantha deserves a dad but I'm tired all the time and look it, so who's going to want me?" She shook her head and sighed. "I just can't get enough damn sleep. I lay in bed worrying about raising Samantha as a single parent, worrying if I have enough money to make ends meet. All the while, knowing my body is having difficulty recovering from my surgery. It's like I can't find the key to turn my brain off. My doctor told me I won't heal properly if I don't manage more sleep."

We sat in silence without looking at each other.

A customer arrived and Samantha woke up so I took her for a walk around the art show. An artist from Oregon had his brilliant animal sculptures on display. Samantha was enthralled examining the artist's work because each sculpture seemed to be a three-dimensional snapshot of the animal subject in motion. This provided us with lots of conversation on exactly what behavior each animal might be engaging in. Samantha obviously inherited her mother's fascination with the natural world. I bought her a twenty-four-inch-tall sculpture of a trio of Brown Pelicans in flight.

We returned to Joan's booth and found her packing up her paintings.

"You want help packing up?" he asked.

Samantha said to Meyer, "Open the box so my mom can see my new sculpture. Joan peered in the box then scowled at Meyer. "No...No way. This is too expensive. Take it back."

"Mom, I like it."

"She brightened my day," Meyer said in an angry and measured tone, "so it's worth it."

"What if she thinks costly gifts should be a normal part of her life." Hands on hips, Joan slowly shook her head. "You don't just show up and upset my world."

"Upset...I bought her a sculpture and asked if you want help packing."

She shook her head. "I'm sorry. There's no future for us. My whole world is this little girl. That's all I have time for. There is no place for you in our world. If I need a man, I'll manage someone." She boxed a painting and put it in her car, turned to me, and said, "You have your own wounds to heal. Find someone who has the time to help you." Joan turned away...began stacking her paintings in the car.

"You want help packing?"

Without looking at me, she said, "I'm worn out. Yea. Please help."

Her car filled, she suggested, "You should at least join us for dinner, for all the help you gave us today."

"I won't be invading your world?"

"You're invited for dinner. Nothing more."

I followed her to a three-bedroom townhouse located in a row of identical townhouses. She parked inside the garage. We moved her artwork from the car to shelves in the garage.

"All I have are leftovers," she said.

"Fine with me."

Samantha approached. "Will you open my sculpture and put it in my room?"

"Samantha..." Joan began but was interrupted by me.

"Right now, little lady. Show me your room."

• • • •

I OFFERED TO HELP WITH dinner, but Joan insisted she wanted to do it by herself.

Joan served blackened salmon over a Greek salad with an amazing raspberry-lemon vinaigrette dressing. The passage of time had certainly not dulled Joan's culinary skills. The meal was an absolute delight.

"Thanks. Lovely meal."

"Why are you leaving?" Samantha said. "Didn't we have fun today?"

"We did but I don't live here and I just came for dinner."

"I have more books you can read me."

Distant thunder boomed a warning.

Joan nodded toward the thunder and said, "Bad storm coming according to the weatherman. Maybe you should stay?"

"I'll sleep on the couch."

"In the morning, you leave."

• • • •

I RETURNED TO THE COUCH after helping Joan clean up and put away dishes. I was laying on my side with my head on the big padded armrest when Samantha came in wearing pajamas and holding her new book.

"I'm going to read to you," she said in a motherly tone, "because you had nice manners at the dinner table."

She read her new book to me and then scampered off to find another book for me to read to her.

It started to rain. The wind picked up as the rain was noisily beating against the windows and sides of the house. Joan came into the living room and sat at the other end of the couch. She started reading when I noticed she positioned herself so our feet and legs were touching, reminding me of when we were reading at the cabin many years before. Distant thunder boomed a warning.

Joan came to attention. "Samantha hates the thunder. She won't sleep tonight if it gets loud."

Samantha heard the thunder too and she came running into the living room with a child-size pillow under one arm and dragging a pink blanket with red satin binding in the other.

"I'm staying with you guys," she informed us.

Joan quietly said we could put Samantha in her own bed after she fell asleep—assuming the thunderstorm passed by.

Samantha put her little pillow on the couch in front of me and then climbed up with her blanket. She asked me to read to her from my book, and as I was reading a book on topology, she was soon fast asleep. But then lightning struck nearby with a powerful *kaboom* and Samantha jumped nearly straight up. I threw my arm around her so she didn't go flying off the couch.

"I don't like thunder noise," she said while pouting.

I explained to her it was loud because of a potential difference of the voltage in the clouds and the ground—the lightening had heated up the air so it expanded quickly and made loud noise.

"Okay—but I still don't like it."

She lay down again, but this time on her side facing away from me. I tucked her blanket completely around her, but she pushed one arm out from the blanket's tight wrap and with her little hand held onto my wrist. There was more thunder, wind, and rain, but Samantha slept through it nestled into my lap.

About ten o'clock the electricity went out. Joan and I talked for a bit and then she took one of the small pillows from the couch and put it on the side of my hip. Lying on her side, she put her head on the pillow, then in the same way as many years before, she wrapped herself around my legs, pulled a blanket over us and went to sleep.

I was reminded of a great line from the movie *When Harry Met Sally*. Harry says, "When you realize you want to spend the rest of your life with somebody, you want the rest of your life to start as soon as possible."

When Samantha was sent to her room to get dressed the next morning, Joan made coffee. They sat on tall chair at her kitchen counter. She said Samantha was a shy and clingy child who never wanted to be out of her mother's view. Even when Joan took her to the children's story group at the library, Joan couldn't wander around the library. She had to stay where Samantha could see her. Joan said she tried putting her in daycare, but Samantha just cried all day.

"She never would sit on anyone else's lap but mine. And she never, *ever* lets anyone else hold her hand."

"Samantha took my hand when we started over to the bookstore."

Joan smiled at me for a few seconds, wrapped her hand around my wrist, and said softly, "She feels it you know. She feels it just the way I did when we were young."

"What does she feel?"

"Remember in junior high, the first time we danced a slow dance and you held me tight against you? I loved the feeling of our bodies touching. I danced slow dances with other guys, and having my body against theirs felt great, but it was different with you. I know we were just junior high kids, but I felt safe and secure with you holding me. I remember thinking I didn't want the feeling to ever end. My daughter sensed that as soon as you met.

She smiled warmly and squeezed my wrist. "During our week at the cabin, when we were getting to know each other, physically, I remember thinking the times we were just reading or sitting together in front of the fireplace were always so precious. I felt peaceful and secure—we were always somehow touching, even when reading at opposite ends of the big swing on the porch."

I sat quietly and gazed into her eyes.

"I always tried to make sure at least our feet were touching—remember the big overstuffed chair in front of the fireplace at the cabin? Instead of sitting on it, I always asked you to sit on the floor with your back against it so I could sit between your legs with my back and head leaning against your chest. I always loved it when you brought your knees up on either side of me so I could wrap my arms around your legs while we sat together—and of course I could easily lean back for a kiss any time I wanted one. I felt complete when we were touching. I'd wake up in the middle of the night and you'd still be holding me. I couldn't tell you then, but I cried one night, as it was so beautiful that you held me."

She looked deep into my eyes. "I'll be honest. When we went off to college and during the time after my sister recovered from the car accident, I had a number of guys—but the secure feeling was never there. When I watched Samantha grab your hand and confidently walk off without me, I was shocked. It was as if a little switch in her head flipped. She knew she was safe. Then afterwards, she not only sat in your lap and read to you, but fell asleep. During the thunderstorm, when I watched her fall asleep on the couch holding your arm, I was certain she felt it. When I was a little girl I knew there was no safer place than my dad's lap, and it appears Samantha absolutely gets the same feeling from you. When we all shared the couch last night, I slept the entire night for the first time in years—even with my head on your bony hip. Thank you."

"I loved it."

She leaned over and kissed me. Her face turned sad. "I need to talk to you about the time after my parents died."

"No, you don't. I mean you can if you want to, but the Lord decided what would be best for us then. Believe me, I wasn't exactly a happy camper when I came home from the army. You might not have wanted to be around me then."

"Maybe it would have been better if we were together then."

"Maybe, but we'll never know for sure. We don't always know why something happens in our lives, but it looks to me as if He's put us together again and I'm happy as hell."

Joan grabbed my hand and squeezed it tightly. "I'm happy as hell about it too." She grinned.

Just then, Samantha raced into the room wanting to know what we were going to do today.

"I think we should go see a Labor Day parade if you and your mom want to,"

Joan agreed. "We can make a picnic lunch and visit a park."

Samantha enthusiastically showed her agreement by bouncing up and down.

I needed to shower first, so Joan sent me to her bathroom. I was just stepping out when she knocked on the bathroom door and came in carrying towels. She was wearing a white terrycloth robe and her ever present scarf was neatly wrapped around her head. She quietly closed the door; taking one of the towels she started wiping the water off my body. She dropped the towel on the floor, looking down at her feet.

Her voice quivering, she said, "I want you to see what I look like now."

She took off her scarf revealing a nearly bald head with peach-fuzz, short blond hair. Then, still looking down at her feet, she untied her robe letting it fall open revealing an angry-looking scar where her right breast had been.

I'm not sure why, but I leaned over and kissed her scar, and then kissed her neck, and then her cheek, and finally her soft lips. "Joan, you're still beautiful to me."

She fastened her arms around my neck as if she would never let go. As I held her tightly, I realized the feeling of wanting to protect her had come back—full force. She slid one of her hands between my legs and began caressing me.

I looked at her with surprise, but she clearly understood what he was thinking.

"Samantha's watching a video," she replied to my unasked question. "Her favorite. She'll be busy for at least twenty minutes. Now, sit on the floor."

I did, and she took me inside her, wrapping her legs and arms around me. I told her I loved her.

She put her warm hand on my cheek, gave me a huge smile, and replied softly, "I know."

• • • •

SAMANTHA AND I VOTED for a quick fast food breakfast, which Joan didn't approve of, but didn't want to be late for the parade.

It was great—lots of marching bands, antique tractors, with the local dance, karate and soccer clubs marching down the street—and seeing as this was an election year, lots of politicians were out pleading for votes.

While Samantha collected candy the politicians were giving out she remarked, "This is almost as good as Halloween."

As I helped Samantha get belted into my pickup truck she told me she thought I must be awfully funny because her mom smiled and laughed so much when I was around. We went to my house after the parade so I could change into clean clothes.

My tri-level home was on the side of a hill leading down to a large lake. The street level met the house at the top floor, so you couldn't see the lower two floors from the street side. Joan became quiet as we walked up to the house. She and Samantha followed me down the top floor hallway to my office where I ran a one-man business from my home.

"This place..." Joan began.

"Has two more floors under this one."

I learned later, Joan thought many of the walls were dripping with testosterone from the way I decorated the place—lots of black, red, chrome and glass. I hadn't even decorated or furnished the lowest level which led out to the covered patio and swimming pool.

My office looked out over the lake and Samantha was pleased to see all the cruising boats. Joan noticed there was a pier leading from the back of my property to a couple of boats.

"Are those yours?"

I told her they were and I had taken the big one on the inside passage to Alaska over a period of a couple of months the previous spring. The smaller one was good for simple overnight trips.

"What does a boat like that big one cost?"

"Just under four million."

"Damn," Joan said.

I took them on a tour of the rest of the house. Joan was quiet and Samantha didn't seem too impressed until she saw the bathtub in the master suite.

"Mom, you could swim in this!"

I made lunch for them by poaching a piece of sushi fresh blue fin tuna. I quickly made it into tuna salad with some finely chopped celery, shallots, and homemade walnut oil mayo, which I plated over a spring mix salad. After lunch, Joan put Samantha down for a nap and joined me on the balcony off the room where Samantha was sleeping. She sat on an adjacent chaise lounge, looking out over the lake.

"This is quite a place. It must impress the girls you bring here."

"It's great, but lonely...and I never bring dates here. As soon as they see this place, I'm never sure if they are interested in the house or me. I own a condo close to downtown which I use when I have meetings in the city—that's where I usually take dates. And here I am," I shrugged, "still single."

Joan moved to sit on my lap. "We've started on different lives, Mr. Minkowski. I'm a single mom. I have huge medical problems and huge medical bills. For the next five years I'll be scared to death every time I visit my doctor's office to see if the cancer has returned." She looked away. "Also I could be sterile from all the treatments."

"Yes, but when we combine our lives your debts will be taken care of and Samantha will have a dad. If money can help the medical problems, that's what it's there for. More importantly, you'll have a partner to help you through whatever comes along. I learned a long time ago that the things I own are merely a reflection of my financial success. Nothing else. Except for donations to charity, it doesn't make me happier. My trip up the inside passage to Alaska was spectacular. I was lucky enough to visit one of the most beautiful parts of the planet and I didn't have anyone to share it with. How sad is that? How *incredibly* sad is that?"

She nodded.

"The large boat has an office and a satellite link so I can still conduct business while on the water. I'm going to keep working when the three of us see Alaska from our own boat. I bought the boat for family trips—not just Meyer trips. Can you imagine the joy we will experience sharing the sights of the inside passage with Samantha? Joan, it is so beautiful—the sea, the mountains, the fjords, the glaciers, the seals, the whales, the sea birds, the golden eagles, and the bald eagles." I sighed. "I know, from the bottom of my heart, sharing a trip with the two of you will be one of the highlights of my entire life."

"I have my own business. I can't just leave it."

"I spend a fortune on tax accountants. I'll buy out your business and you come to work with me."

Joan spoke in an almost frightened tone, "This is too much change. You're thinking way ahead of me. We both have been through so much. I know I care about you, but I just can't commit to changing my life so completely."

I tried to reassure her. "I think like an engineer. I'm a problem-solving kind of guy. I have no doubt we can solve nearly anything that comes along, as long as we're together."

"I hear what you're saying, but I just can't be as certain. You're miles ahead of me."

"It's okay for now. You'll catch up."

Joan stared at me for a bit, kissed my cheek, and then put her head on my shoulder as we watched the boats cruising on the lake. An hour later we were startled by the sound of percussion instruments.

"Samantha is awake and discovered my drum room."

• • • •

AS WE WERE LEAVING my house, Samantha noticed my Sabbath candleholders. "You can't do candle lighting," she said. "It's only for ladies to do."

"So you must come to my house next Friday for Sabbath dinner to light my candles for me."

"Okay. Mom?" Samantha turned enthusiastically toward her mother.

"Sounds good to me." Joan beamed at her daughter and secretly poked me in the ribs. "Do you always try to get dates by inviting your potential date's daughter to dinner?"

"Only for Sabbath!"

The next Friday Joan and I proceeded down to the wine cellar to find a kosher wine for Sabbath dinner.

"This is a cosy location. The little glass topped table with the wrought iron frame and matching chairs fits the decor. It feels like a little garden in here. Do you know about all the wines here?"

"I knew most of them."

I pointed out the back wall of the wine cellar moved and there was another room behind it. She asked if she could see it and I opened it by entering a ten-digit pin into a hidden keypad. As the wall moved to the side, a light went on revealing my extensive pistol and rifle collection.

"I don't know about this," Joan said.

I tried to assure her this was a safe way to store guns and besides, she hadn't been in the shooting range yet.

"Whoa, we need to talk. I don't like this. Samantha's an awfully small child to be in a home with all these guns—let alone a shooting range."

"You've already walked past the entrance to the range three times and didn't see it. It has a twelve-character password to get in, even if you did see the entrance. I learned from my father it was important to know how to shoot because my family was worth protecting, even if it cost me my life. I seem to remember you were the beneficiary of Dad's teachings some years ago."

She nodded, smiled, and kissed me. "Yes. I vividly remember how terrified I was when I saw that bear running toward me, but then I saw you standing on the deck of the cabin with a rifle against your shoulder. You appeared so calm; like shooting a running bear was something you did all the time. I was still scared, but I had little doubt you would do whatever it took to protect me. And you did."

We found a Cabernet Blanc with overtones of pear and a hint of persimmon. Those flavors and its smooth finish complemented the fresh salmon dinner we had prepared together. We began our Sabbath celebration with Joan and Samantha each lighting candles and chanting the blessing.

I chanted the blessing over the wine then suggested, "We should sing the Shehechianu because I'm certain this would be the first of many Sabbath dinners we would be celebrating together. It also thanks God for allowing us to arrive at this day." I could see tears forming in Joan's eyes as we sang the beautiful prayer together.

Samantha recited the blessing over the lovely Sabbath *Challah* Joan had baked. Each tore a piece off the *Challah*, dipped it in salt, and ate it. Joan said Samantha participated in Sabbath as soon as she was big enough to help, making Sabbath special for both of them. Samantha even told me a little about this week's *Parsha*—Bible reading.

As we began eating our soup, followed by Joan's homemade gefilte fish, Joan and I debated the lessons to be learned from the *Parsha*.

"This is as special as our first Sabbath in the cabin," Joan told me.

"As soon as I saw you at the mall, I prayed the connection between us was still there."

The first Sabbath together meant so much to us because we were celebrating it as a family. Even the candles seemed to glow brighter than usual.

When Joan walked into the room with pumpkin pie for dessert, Samantha surprised us by saying, "Meyer, you're going to enjoy this pumpkin pie. It has minnows baked in it." And then she laughed her melodic laugh. My house was finally becoming a home as it filled with Joan and Samantha's laughter.

After dinner we all read in the family room. Joan read a story to Samantha about Miriam. Then when Joan and I went to bed we performed the requisite Sabbath *Mitzvah*—a couple of times, as it happens.

Chapter Seven ~ Prelude to a Real Long Kiss

A COUPLE MONTHS LATER, on a cool, fall Northwest day, Joan and Javier, my gardener, were cleaning up some of the flower beds around my yard. There was a light breeze coming off the lake and large cumulus clouds glided across the sky, occasionally blocking out the sun.

Although Javier was being paid to take care of the gardens Joan found it therapeutic to have her hands involved in gardening and insisted on helping. She was looking and feeling much better than when I had first ran into her at the mall—she had so much more strength. We began working out together each morning during her weekend visits to my home.

She reported to her doctor that she no longer needed her sleeping pills. He asked what had changed and she told him she was in the best relationship of her life.

Her doctor told her, "Isn't love grand?"

I couldn't help but wonder if the garden would become Joan's new canvas. The world seemed to brighten for her when working with plants.

While her mother and Javier worked, Samantha was busy helping them with her own child-sized garden tools and wheelbarrow and when I had finished some work in my office I joined them outside.

I took out a hoe and loosened the soil in a loamy eight-foot by two-foot flower bed. I had a bag of spring bulbs and yelled to Samantha, asking if she could help me.

She ran over to me with her little hoe on her shoulder. I started to tell her not to run when holding garden tools, but her mom beat me to it.

It was getting late in the afternoon and the temperature was dropping. Samantha's cheeks were getting rosy from the cool air as I had her write her name on a small board. I added an apostrophe 's' and printed the word garden after it. I attached the board to a stake and placed it at the edge of the flower bed.

"Now it's officially your garden."

I showed Samantha a picture of the flowers that would grow from the bulbs we were planting. "After the bulbs come up in the spring, we will plant more flowers and some carrots in your garden."

We worked side by side and I showed her how to place the bulbs in the depression I had cut in the soil and taught her how the bulbs needed to be right side up.

"Are we going to cover them up with dirt?" Samantha asked.

I said yes.

"But how will they know which way is up?"

"Gravity will tell them."

"You can't feel gravity," she informed me.

So I picked her up and threw her into the air and caught her. "See, gravity brought you back down to me or you would be headed to the moon by now. Did you feel it?"

"I'm not sure. Ummm...maybe you should send me up there again so I can check."

I kept throwing her up in the air until my arms ached and Joan accused us of goofing off.

"We are certainly not goofing off." I thought for a bit then added, "We're performing a science experiment."

She and Javier looked at each other and laughed hysterically.

I heard Javier tell Joan in his thick accent, "Mr. Meyer he's more happier now you visit. Before you and Samantha coming over, him quiet and angry. And he no smile so much. I tell him one time, why you want to be alone in this big house, but he no answer. But now you and Samantha is coming over, dat big house; it fit you family. I know now, he have dat big house waiting for a *familia*. Sometime he look at you guys and he smile big—I think his head going to break. He so *happy* now."

Joan smiled at him sweetly.

After a pause, Javier continued. "And Mr. Meyer, he sure adores *la pequeña*, Samantha."

"I know," Joan said. "And she adores Meyer. She's loath to disappoint him. If she says something nasty to me, Meyer gives her that look of his and she knows immediately that he is upset with her—and she's just crushed. And if Meyer tells her that her behavior hurt someone's feelings, that's good for a fifteen-minute cry. She can't wait until the weekends when we can spend time here. She even calls him after her storytelling group at the library each weekday morning, so she can tell him about the story she heard that day. He was in a meeting with a client on Thursday when she called him. He interrupted the meeting to talk to her. One day she decided to draw a picture about the story she heard so she could give it to Meyer the following weekend. With all the expensive art in his house, he emptied an entire wall near the entry to make space for Samantha's artwork."

"Well, you know," Javier said with a big grin on his face. "That's what fathers do."

I smiled at Javier's words. He was in my corner.

Javier left for the day and we all went into the house to clean up. Joan brought up what Javier had said about fathers.

"Well, I'm not really her father," I reminded her. "I mean, you haven't caught up to my thinking about our future as a family yet."

"Okay. Okay. I give up. I surrender." She slid her arms around me, caressing the back of my neck. "I, without any doubt or reservation, want to spend the rest of my life with you, Meyer Minkowski."

Samantha looked at us confused.

While gazing at me with an expression of love, plus one hand still on the back of my neck and the other around my waist, Joan said, "Samantha, we have to start planning a wedding."

"Great! That will be fun. Who's getting married?"

• • • •

AROUND DINNER TIME I made an announcement. "I think we should have some Champagne tonight."

Joan looked at a grinning Samantha and appeared as if she thought we might be up to something.

I poured champagne for myself and Joan and ginger ale in a champagne glass for Samantha. She could barely contain her excitement. "Go ahead, Mom, drink your champagne."

Joan clearly suspected a trick. As I handed her a champagne flute, I concealed the bottom of the stem with my hand. Then as she took her champagne, she noticed the engagement ring tied to the stem with a bright pink ribbon. Her jaw dropped then she smiled.

"Joan, will you marry me?"

She was too busy crying to answer, she just nodded, and I put the ring on her finger. We embraced and shared a long kiss.

"You guys kiss too much," a mildly disgusted looking Samantha said.

At dinner that night Joan explained to Samantha, "When Meyer and I get married you and I would live here with him. We would move all of our things over here."

"Everything?" Samantha asked.

"Everything that we wanted to keep," Joan reassured her.

I asked Samantha, "Do you want to live here?"

"Well, that might be okay. I like my room here, and I like being close to the lake, but I don't like your library."

I couldn't believe she said that. I was devastated. My library was a large, two story room with walnut paneling, floor to ceiling book shelves, plus a Hickory and Brazilian cherry wood trimmed circular stairway to the upper level. Architectural Digest came to take pictures of it. It was the part of the house that I was most proud of and took the most time to design when I built it. If that room couldn't put you in a mood to read or study, nothing could.

"What don't you like?"

She elaborated. "All the chairs are too big and it doesn't have a desk my size so I can draw pictures. And it doesn't have a shelf that I can reach to put my books on."

Now, that made more sense. I solemnly promised by the next time she visited there would be Samantha-sized furniture and shelves in that room.

In the middle of dinner that night, a realization coalesced in Samantha's mind. Her eyes grew large and a broad smile spread across her face. Samantha looked at her mom, and at maximum volume she screamed, "When you marry Meyer, I'm gonna have a dad!"

Later that evening, after Samantha had gone to bed and the Sabbath candles had burned out, Joan and I proceeded outside to one of the balconies overlooking the lake. I poured a glass of wine for each of us and we cuddled together in the cool evening air, wrapped in a Pendleton *Chief Joseph* blanket. It's a bright, colorful, warm, and soft blanket and even when the late-evening breeze picked up it didn't penetrate the blanket and take away the warmth we'd created by being wrapped around each other.

I asked Joan if there was anything special she wanted me to do when she and Samantha moved in.

In a serious tone she told me, "Well, you have to promise to hold me every night just the same way you did when we were at the cabin. I know you do that now but that must continue. Whenever we're reading you have to position yourself so that we're touching—and there have to be lots of evenings where we just sit and hold each other."

"Is that all?"

"No," Joan smiled, "we have to find things to laugh about every day."

"Oh man, I knew it was going to be tough to be your husband, but I didn't think you would be so demanding—but for you and Samantha I guess I'll have to manage."

In actuality I subscribed to the same family happiness philosophy as my father. To wit: If the wife is happy, then the family is happy. With Joan as my partner, all I had to do is make sure we did things as a family and she would be happy and therefore our family would be happy.

• • • •

THE NEXT DAY JOAN BROUGHT over a carload of her paintings. I had cleared a wall at the entry, opposite the wall I had set up for Samantha's artwork.

"I painted this when I was a junior in college." Joan opened a box and pulled out a large painting. "The assignment was to paint a childhood memory. I agonized for days over which memory to depict. The day before the assignment was due; stood in front of a blank six-foot-wide by four-foot-tall canvas, struggling for an idea. And then, as if a flood gate opened, the entire painting cascaded into my mind."

Her hands made sweeping gestures around the canvas as she spoke. "I painted this huge, black X from corner to corner. My paintbrush seemed to have a mind of its own—in the upper triangle, I painted this young boy and girl on their knees intently staring into a stream to see the minnows that swam there. Then here, on the right, the same young people painting scenery and assembling model railroad cars. In this lower triangle, they are wrapped around each other while they dance slowly at a junior high dance. The left-hand triangle has a group of adults leaving a train platform while one little girl has turned back to wave to a friend who is still on the train."

Her eyes glanced quickly at me then back at the canvas. "I've never put it on display to sell. It has spent most of its existence in this box, but now that we're together again...I want the spirit of our long-ago childhood and train trip to be the center of the art space."

On a two-dimensional surface, she had captured the joyous spirit of our childhood. I lifted the painting and hung it in the center of her space. More times than I can count, I look at that painting, feeling surrounded by our childhood experiences.

I took her by the hand. "I have some things for you to see in my storage room." A few lights turned on in the storage room and I pulled a poster-board-sized box out of a corner and took a shoebox down from a shelf. As I opened the shoebox, Joan smiled when she saw it was full of index cards.

"My mom saved these for me. These are the index cards from our visits to the library."

"This is great. I can make a collage out of these."

"My folks insisted that I save them."

From the larger box I pulled out the poster boards that Joan had painted for the scenic background for our basement railroad.

Her eyes opened wide as she saw the old poster boards.

"My mom also packed up all the cars, buildings, and scenery."

"Oh wow," Joan kept saying as I opened a large carton and carefully unwrapped one Joan-decorated and Meyer-built car or structure after another. It was as if I was unpacking little pieces of our childhood that we could see and hold in our hands.

With joy radiating from her face, and her hands on my shoulders, she decisively declared, "You're going to have to make some room, baby. The Joan-Meyer-Meyer-Joan Railroad is coming back to life."

I replicated the train table my father created for us and gradually the JMMJ Railroad did start coming back to life. Whenever we wanted an indoor project with no time pressure to finish, we would create more scenes on our miniature railroad. With modern electronics and lighting, I seemed to be continually wiring tiny lights in buildings and railroad cars. Years later we could run the railroad at night without turning on the room lights. And the audio she insisted on—don't get me started on the audio.

Someplace along the line I realized, even as adults, it didn't matter what Joan and I were doing or where we were doing it. As long as we were doing it together, we were happy. Happy, in our vocabulary, means laughing and loving each other, plus finding joy in each other's accomplishments and the accomplishments of our children.

A few weeks before our wedding Joan told me, "Samantha has a question for you. We've been talking about it and I've decided to let the two of you work it out."

I crouched down to Samantha's level. "When can I call you Dad?" she asked with a look of anticipation spreading across her face.

I'd been thinking about that as well. While I was obviously developing a father-daughter relationship with Samantha, I wasn't her biological father. I was concerned about this, as I didn't want Sam's memory to be forgotten. I had already planned to visit the Vietnam Memorial Wall when Samantha was older so she could see Sam's name on the wall.

"Well, it's your choice," I told her. "When you feel comfortable calling me dad then that's when you should call me dad. It would be a huge honor that you would want to call me that. But we're not going to forget your birth dad."

"So, it's my choice?"

"Yes, it's your—"

"Okay, Dad!"

I scooped her up and she wrapped her little arms around my neck. I held her tightly—in part because of the bonding moment we had just shared, but truthfully, also because I didn't want her to see the tears in my eyes.

The wedding was a wonderful affair. Not just because of the food or the decorations, or even the people that came—but because I was finally joining my life with Joan's, and little Samantha's too, of course. Now, truthfully, as much as I like to think I have a way with words, I decided that Samantha herself would be the best choice to describe the festivities.

The following are her words, her recollections, and I promised her I would write them as she dictated them.

• • • •

WELL, FINALLY MY MOM and Meyer were married today! Mom awakened me early and told me to shower and brush my teeth really good so I would have a pretty smile. Outside in our backyard, they set things up in front of the lake. They had a big white tent with the sides rolled up over the covered swimming pool and some men and ladies set up chairs and tables in there. Mom said we would have dinner in there after the ceremony.

Nathan Rifkin is at the wedding too, but I don't like him—he's a boy! Except that he's the son of Dad's first cousin, Dov, so Mom said I should be nice to him. He's a few years older than me, and his father is a Rabbi. Nathan talks to his mom in a language called Yiddish and to his dad in a language called Hebrew. I can't understand either of the languages, so I just talk to them in plain old English.

Nathan comes by our house after supper a couple times a week to learn algebra from Dad. My mom studies Torah with Nathan's dad then too, and he was teaching me the Hebrew alphabet also. They said Nathan's a math prodigy. I think that means he's really good with numbers. Dad and Nathan seem to have lot of fun playing *algebra* together.

My mom dressed me in my flower-girl dress, shoes, and hat. The dress was as white as the snow on Mt. Rainier and came all the way down to my ankles. It was super long and it had a big pink sash and I able to wear white shoes and a big white hat with a wide brim. There was also a wide pink ribbon on the hat that hung below the brim in the back and I even wore white gloves.

Now, my job was to walk slowly up the aisle between all the people and drop flower petals that my mom was going to walk on. We had a rehearsal yesterday and it was awful. Everybody kept telling me I was walking too fast and I was getting sad, but Dad said not to worry. He said that we would work something out later. We did.

At the wedding I held the flower basket by its handle in my left hand just like they showed me, and I walked up the aisle, the way everyone said I should. But halfway up the aisle, Dad raised one of his eyebrows at me—that was the signal.

Dad taught me to sing one of my favorite songs in my head and move to the beat. So, from halfway up the aisle to the end, in my head I was singing "Sweet Home Chicago." Dad and I had practiced some great dancing steps. He said I could get my groove on. So all the rest of the way up the aisle, while I was tossing flower petals, I was moving and dancing and doing some spins that Dad showed me. That way everyone could see that I could keep my groove on.

At the front, I did my last spin right in front of Dad. We high fived just like we practiced. My dad is so cool for teaching me to do that stuff. Everyone was smiling, so I guess I did okay. My mom came up the aisle next and she took forever. She walked so slowly. I think I should tell her to walk to a faster song next time, so she doesn't take so long.

The rabbi stood in front of my mom and dad—my very own dad! All three of them were under a *Chuppa*—that's a wedding canopy by the way—Mom and Dad designed and built it together. Over the top of the *Chuppa*, my dad had spread out his new *Tallis*—and that is a prayer shawl—that my mom bought for him.

I heard them recite the blessing for the wine a couple of times and they had to drink wine from this neat looking *Kiddush* cup. They were smiling a lot, except near the end when my mom was kind of crying and smiling at the same time. I looked around the room and other people, even both my grandparents, were smiling and crying at the same time. I guess that's something you learn to do when you're getting to be a grown up. I think Mom calls them tears of joy, 'cause she does it sometimes when I do something really, really nice for her.

The ceremony took a while. I was supposed to sit with my grandparents, but it was boring, so I kept my groove on and kept on moving to the music in my head. At the end of the ceremony they had this really, really long kiss. I mean, *really long*—and right in front of everybody! My mom and dad didn't seem to care about that, but Nathan and I were both giggling at them. Then dad broke a glass under his shoe and everybody yelled, "*Mazel Tov!*" and we all sang "*Simin Tov* and *Mazel Tov*" which is one of my all-time favorite songs.

After we ate dinner, there was dancing. My mom and dad danced first, then Mom danced with Dad's dad, and Dad danced with me. It was a slow song that Dad called a waltz, but I didn't know how to dance slowly so Dad had me stand on the tops of his shoes so that way we both moved together. It was fun. After that, Dad danced with his mom and then I saw Nathan coming over to me. He asked me to dance with him. I didn't want to, but out of the corner of my eye I saw my mom giving me *that* look. You know—the one that said I'd better act nice or the ceiling might fall on my head. I think she learned that from Dad, because he gave *the look* better than anybody did.

So, I said yes to Nathan. I have to say, he was a pretty good dancer, for a boy. I thought he should have asked me if I wanted to stand on his shoes too, but decided that was just for Dad and me.

I had always wondered something, so I asked Nathan. "Why is your older brother always in a wheelchair?"

"He has Cerebral Palsy," he told me. "It means he has trouble controlling his muscles."

"Oh. I'm going to tell my dad about that because I he can fix everything," I said.

Then Nathan smiled at me, a really big smile. "My brother would be awfully happy if he did."

After we danced a couple of times, I told him I was thirsty.

He yelled, "Come on!" and I followed him over to a bar.

"Two martinis, please," he said to the barman.

"Yes, sir!" the barman said.

I couldn't believe it. I was about to have my first martini. Well, that's what I thought. Turns out it was just lime soda with a little cherry juice, but it was served in a martini glass and had a shiny red cherry in it.

"He always gives me this no matter what I order," Nathan told me.

We laughed and pretended we were grownups with real drinks. It was fun.

We were standing near my mom and dad when Nathan said, "Did you know that silvery minnows are a member of the Hypognathous genus in the Cyprinid family? I thought you would want to know because Meyer told me that you have an interest in minnows."

I didn't understand a couple of the words he'd said—but Dad repeated them to me later—anyway, it sounded like Nathan knew what he was talking about, so I thought that was pretty good for a boy to know something about minnows. Nathan didn't seem to be as bad as I had imagined. He could dance and knew about minnows. I'm telling you—not too bad for a boy.

My mom and dad must have overheard what Nathan had said about minnows, because Mom looked at Dad and elbowed him in the side. She said, "I think I'll have to burn the cabin down before those two graduate high school."

Dad thought that was awfully funny, but I didn't get it. Why would they want to burn our cabin down? Oh well, just one of those things grown-ups say that doesn't make any sense.

More of our cousins came over and we went and played some neat games together. Later in the afternoon, the cover was removed from the swimming pool and the real fun began as all the cousins and I went swimming in the pool.

Oh! I almost forgot to tell you about the cake. It was a whole bunch of cakes stacked on top of each other. It was pretty on the outside, but inside it had different flavors of chocolate. I heard someone say the cake was, *Death by Chocolate*, but I don't think that's true because my cousins and I ate a lot of that cake and not even one of us died.

I also heard someone one say there were more desserts than you could shake a stick at. My cousins and I thought that was rather strange, as we couldn't imagine why you would shake a stick at desserts. But I figured I should try, so I found a stick and shook it at a couple of the desserts. Then Mom saw me and gave me the ceiling-might-fall-on-my-head expression. Well that time, the look told me that if I didn't get rid of the stick, two ceilings would fall on my head.

Nathan's dad seemed to be having a lot of fun, though. He was laughing a lot and kept asking the barman for martinis. He hoisted a martini that didn't seem to have the pink color in it, like mine did, and instead of a cherry, he received an olive. Yuk!

I don't think Nathan's mom thought that was a good thing to drink because she told Nathan's dad, if he reached for one more martini, she would unscrew his wrist. Everyone thought that was funny. I didn't know you could unscrew someone's wrist. I better keep reading books. I have a lot to learn.

At the wedding I learned about something called a honeymoon. A honeymoon is really a vacation that the people who just married get to take. They call it a honeymoon because if they call it a vacation, they have to take their kids along.

So my parents went to Mendocino, California after the wedding and I went home to Grandma and *Zaydie's* house. Don't feel too bad that I couldn't go on the honeymoon, because at the wedding *Zaydie* whispered to me that the nectarines in his yard were getting ripe and I could come to their summer home in the Yakima Valley and eat as many nectarines as I was tall. If you haven't had Yakima Valley nectarines, you should know that Dad called them God's greatest summertime gift to humanity. And best of all, *Zaydie* and Grandma would be canning some of the nectarines, and if I helped them, I could have some to take home. That way I could eat them during the winter. Wow!

Grandma and *Zaydie's* kitchen smelled wonderful while they cooked and prepared the nectarines for canning. My job with the canning was to draw a picture of a nectarine on each of the labels that would go on top of the jars. Grandma showed me how to draw a Nectarine, but after I drew a few I started adding some little leaves and a stem. They made them look better, I thought. A couple of times I drew two nectarines on the same stem. My grandparents seemed happy with this. I could tell from their smiles when they looked at my labels. They said something about my being like my mom. I don't think so. My mom is old and I am definitely *not* old.

I took some of my new books from Meyer's, ummm...Dad's...ummm...I mean *our* library to their house to read to my Grandparents. I was amazed that people as old as my grandparents were so interested in my books. They were smiling and looking at me and listening carefully to my reading. That's good because I was sure they learned a lot. My mom tells me you can always learn something new from a book. Gram and *Zaydie* must have been listening and looking at me so carefully because they knew they were going to learn something.

Then, when Mom and Dad returned from Mendocino, they told us about their trip. I heard them tell people that they sat and watched the sun setting over the *Specific* Ocean one evening. How sad for them. All the way down to California and the only thing they had to do was sit and watch the sun go down. Boring! I was glad I was canning nectarines and going for walks at my grandparents' home instead.

So, I also remembered to ask my dad if he could fix Nathan's older brother. He said that he wished that he could. That bothered me. His brother's wheelchair didn't look like a fun place for a kid. Maybe I could figure something out. At least I could try.

Chapter Eight ~ Sailing Takes Us Back

AS I HAD PROMISED, I bought out Joan's business after we were married. It was now the Meyer and Joan Investment Firm and every day when I went to work, Joan was there working with me. With her incredibly sharp mind, she was catching on to my business quite quickly and even discovered things that I hadn't thought of that made my work easier. And best of all, she was my thermometer. She had the uncanny ability to tell me when I was getting angry before I even became aware of it. If I didn't manage to calm down, she would take over the situation for me. What more could a man ask for in a partner.

Sometime in October we decided to take the smaller of my two boats and spend a long weekend in the San Juan Islands. We had been taking Samantha on progressively longer boat rides on the lake in front of my house to get her used to the idea of being as safety conscious as possible for a five-year-old. We practiced lots of emergency drills until we were reasonably certain she would know what to do. We decided on a Thursday to Tuesday trip. It would take about four hours to cruise up there and then we would dock the boat in a harbor and explore the island and cruise around it.

On the Sunday morning before our trip, Joan received a phone call from her grandmother, Esther. She'd been living in Iowa with her younger sister for quite a few years, since Esther's husband, Manny, died.

"She wants to fly out see us," Joan told me with her hand over the phone.

"Fine with me," I told her.

"Grandma, it would be wonderful if you would come out. And yes, we have room here for you to stay with us. I'll have tickets waiting for you at the airport. Grandma, don't worry about the money for the tickets. It's not even an issue," Joan said beaming at me.

After a little pause Joan continued, "Okay Grandma. You can buy groceries for us when you get here."

"Maybe we should put off our boat ride," I offered.

"Let's wait until she gets here. She takes pretty good care of herself. We might be surprised what good shape she's in for someone in their late eighties."

Joan was right about her grandmother. She was in excellent shape physically and mentally.

When Samantha was giving her a tour of our house and showed her our library, Esther told Samantha, "I think I'll tell your mother to move my things in here, because I may never want to leave this room."

I showed her the elevator that was installed in case people who visited our home were in wheelchairs and couldn't negotiate the stairs.

"That's nice of you to have that," she said, "but for me, I want to take the stairs for the exercise."

She was ecstatic when we told her about our planned trip.

"Your grandfather and I took a boat trip to the San Juan Islands a few months after we were married. It was really our honeymoon. Imagine, after all these years I get to visit those beautiful islands again, but with my great-granddaughter and granddaughter. Wherever your grandfather is, he's smiling right now." She stood up. "Where's Samantha? We have to look up what fish, whales, and birds we might see so we can keep a list."

As her grandmother walked away, Joan turned to me. "Think Samantha's going to have a great week with Grandma?"

I smiled. "I think we all will."

• • • •

JUST BEFORE OUR FAMILY boat trip to the San Juan Islands, my parents came in from their summer home in the Yakima Valley.

"Are you ready for inspection, Meyer?" my dad asked.

"Ready as I'll ever be, Dad."

Dad always inspected my boat before I left on a trip and would give me a punch list of things to repair or have inspected. There wasn't much to do, but Dad insisted on helping with the one item that needed repair, tightening a seal on the propeller shaft.

Esther, Joan and my mom were making up a list of supplies to bring on the boat. While we were cruising to the Islands, my parents would be flying to Israel with friends of theirs.

"Dad," Joan asked my father, "did you think Meyer and I were meant to be together."

"I couldn't be sure, but you each did little things to take care of each other that were astounding for children as young as you were. You were both aware of each other's feelings. Remember when we moved to Maple Woods in Washington State. In the middle of the summer, Meyer hurt his ankle. He had to stay off his feet for a day until the swelling went down. You two spent the entire day on the couch in our library. You periodically put more ice in the ice bag that he had to keep on his ankle. You two read to each other the entire day. How many children at ten years of age would do that? Also, I remember the following summer that Meyer read Christina Rossetti's poetry to you when you had your tonsils removed and couldn't talk. He hated poetry then, but was willing to bring your favorite poet's lines to life because of your relationship."

"I remember that," Joan said. "He read her poetry to me with so much feeling, that to this day, when I reread some of those poems, I still hear his voice reciting them to me."

My mom, Joan, and Esther went shopping and loaded all the supplies onto the boat. I drove my parents to the airport that afternoon and gave them eighteen dollars for *Tzedakah* in Israel.

That evening we slept on the boat so I could get our journey to the San Juan Islands under way before the others had awakened. Early the next morning, I checked the oil level in the engines and generators. They rumbled to life with a brief puff of smoke. I checked the oil pressure gauges for each engine and then went out to untie the dock lines. Everything looked good so I put the transmissions in gear.

We proceeded slowly out into the lake and entered the canal that would take us to the locks and into Puget Sound. With the engines at idle, I could maintain five knots, which was just below the maximum for the channel to the locks. I was running the boat from the flybridge.

Fifteen minutes later, Joan came up from the kitchen area with a cup of coffee for each of us. We each had thick sweaters on to ward off the early morning chill. Joan put out bumpers in preparation for entering the locks. Esther and Samantha weren't awake yet. It was a slightly foggy morning, but the sun would quickly burn off the fog to turn it into a beautiful day with clear blue skies. As we sipped our coffee, we motored out of the locks, and I guided our boat into Puget Sound for our ten-hour trip.

Joan asked, "Have you noticed anything about Samantha's reading skills?"

I had but I kept pushing it out of my mind. After considering her question for a while I told her, "You and I were reading at a much higher level by now and reading as much for information as for fun. Samantha just reads for fun and doesn't have our drive to be learning all the time. And she has fun drawing, but doesn't have your talent."

I had Joan take over the helm for a bit while I checked the charts for a navigation reference. Then as I took the helm back, I said, "Did you notice at our wedding when everyone was dancing, Samantha went over to Jonathan's wheelchair and while holding one of his hands, danced with him? She felt bad that no one was dancing with him. And when my cousin, Dov, took Jonathan in the pool, only Samantha played with him. She took a ball over to him. When she saw that he was trying to hold it with his hands, but couldn't bring them together, she put her hands on the backs of his and pushed them together so he could hold the ball. Of all the young cousins, only Samantha has the patience to listen to Jonathan's mangled speech until she understands what he is trying to say. She has complete conversations with him, whenever they're together."

As Joan and I were sharing a bench seat, she put her head on my shoulder. "At Samantha's age you and I would have wanted to know the technical details of Jonathan's condition, but that would have been it for us. We'd never have the patience she has. I've noticed the kids can be mean to Nathan because he's so far ahead of them in school. One little girl was getting a bit carried away with the teasing. Nathan turned to her and said something cruel. Samantha told him, in your tone of voice I might add, that there is never a reason to talk mean. I was waiting for a verbal explosion from Nathan. Instead he quietly told Samantha she was right, then he turned to the girl he had insulted and apologized."

"You don't think they—"

"Have a future as a couple. I doubt it. Samantha is clever, but Nathan is incredibly bright. He'll probably need someone as bright as he is to keep up with him." Joan thought for a minute and continued, "But Nathan did tell me that Samantha should go to his school so he could make sure none of the other kids bothered her."

A wide grin spread across her face. "We may have to burn the cabin down sooner than we planned. I'll tell you what else, after I talked to your father yesterday, I'm certain he knew about us from early on. When we were on the train he seemed to spend a lot of time showing us things. He sent the two of us off to the dining car for a sundae, as if we were a couple. He made sure we sat next to each other at all the meals."

"You may be right. Remember when we had that big argument? He didn't waste time trying to see who was at fault. Instead he told us, 'both of you should be ashamed of yourselves to let your friendship end up in an argument. Each of you owes the other one an apology and I better never hear unkind words from either of you.'"

I sipped my coffee and pondered. "Come to think of it, my dad always made sure you had enough art supplies at my house so that we could keep working on our model railroad. Oh my God...I was continually building things and you were busy decorating and painting the things I had built. Remember? He would stop us every now and then to make sure we were planning together what would come next. After a while, I wouldn't buy anything for the model railroad unless you and I discussed it. He saw that we were good for each other and continually put us in situations where we had to learn to get along and grow together. How many other fourth and fifth graders could have done that? He must have at least suspected."

"I agree," Joan exclaimed. "Whenever we had a disagreement over what you should build or how I should paint something, we would ask him and he would listen to each of us and then suggest how we could resolve our differences. I didn't realize it then, but he never made the decision for us, but taught us how to resolve it ourselves—as a couple. Remember, when your parents invited my parents over to their house to see the railroad. I was surprised my mom and dad wanted *you* to show them what we constructed. I'll bet they just wanted to get to know who was making their daughter so happy."

"I didn't know until recently that the summer we drove to the cabin, it was my dad's idea that we take the Corvette. My mother told him that it was dangerous to let me drive that powerful little car, but Dad told her, 'With Joan in the car, there was no way Meyer would do anything to put her in danger.' Of course, he was right."

"And that brings us to Nathan and Samantha."

"What does?" Samantha ran up the stairs and into the pilot-house.

Joan replied to her with lines from Lewis Carroll's *The Walrus and the Carpenter*. "'The time has come,' the Walrus said. 'To talk of other things. Of shoes and ships and sealing-wax. Of cabbages and kings. And why the sea is boiling hot. And whether pigs have wings.'"

"Sometimes you guys are strange," Samantha told us.

"What do you think of Nathan?" Joan asked.

"He's nice, Mom, but he's a boy, and you know about boys."

"Didn't he bring a book over to show you which whales, seals, and sea otters you might see during our trip?" I said.

"Yes, and that was nice, but then we argued. Remember, Dad? You interrupted us and said that we owed each other an apology and you never wanted to hear us talking to each other with such unkind words."

"Oh really," Joan said. "We certainly may have to burn that cabin down sooner than we planned."

"Good morning, all," Esther called to us from the main deck. "I am making Rainier cherry blintzes for breakfast, if anyone wants."

"I'll help," said Joan.

"Me too," yelled Samantha and followed Joan down to the kitchen area.

After breakfast, Joan and Esther sat in the pilothouse while Samantha and I went out on deck to look for whales and seals. After a while Samantha was tired and laid down for a rest so I joined Joan and her grandmother where they were sitting and chatting.

Over the next week, in between whale, eagle, and bear sightings, Joan and I learned about Manny and Esther Weiss. The following is her story as she told it to me.

Chapter Nine ~ Esther and Manny Weiss

I WAS BORN IN 1895 in the capital of Romania. I was named Esther, after my mother's sister who died when she was young. We came across the ocean to New York City in a big ship when I was eight. My father and brothers crossed before us and sent money for my mother, sister, and me to come to the US. We didn't come over first class believe me. We slept with my feet in my sister's face and her feet in mine. My sister, Shifrah, and I thought it was so funny. I was sure it was awful for the adults, but we were little girls and didn't know better.

When we arrived in New York, there were people with the letters HIAS on signs, standing for Hebrew Immigrant Aid Society, at the dock to greet us. None of us spoke English yet so it was a blessing to get some help. They directed us to the train station so we could ride the rails to Chicago. When we arrived, we took a second train to Iowa, and when we arrived at that train station my father was there to greet us.

"Miriam! Over here," he yelled to us.

"Avram! Here we are," Momma yelled back.

Momma was so excited to see him. She was so happy I don't think her feet touched the ground for the next two weeks. We moved into the little apartment over Papa's dry-goods store and Momma began turning it from a little apartment into a warm home for all of us.

On Friday night when Momma was blessing the candles, Papa became teary eyed and could hardly recite the blessing for the wine. He was so happy Momma and his daughters were finally living with him. Naturally we sang *Shehechianu* in honor of our first Sabbath together in our new home.

Papa's brothers were there as well. You wouldn't believe how many times they thanked my mother for inviting them. I think that was partly because that Sabbath dinner was one of the few home cooked meals they had eaten since they arrived in Iowa.

Mother organized her household duties into a routine and then began visiting the store. "Looking at it with a woman's eye," Papa told us later.

She noticed that, while a lot of women shopped in Papa's store, he didn't have the bolts of cloth and sewing materials displayed in a manner that made it enticing for women to buy. She told papa to put the bolts of cloth in the front window and she made a dress from some of the cloth and hung it there.

Soon Papa was selling quite a bit of cloth and Mama was being asked to sew dresses for some of the store's clients. While Mama had no time to make clothing for someone else's family, she was always the business woman. She asked Lena, a widowed Italian friend who loved to sew, to come and sew clothing for Papa's shop. Within a couple of years, the dress shop took up so much space and made so much money, Papa and his brothers built a small store by itself. Mama named the dress store Lena and Miriam's Frocks. The two of them became great friends and remained so all their lives.

Jews were an integral part of our little community on the Mississippi River. A Rabbi came to our little town once a month and each Sabbath, one of the families had services in their home.

As I grew, I had a never-ending curiosity that I satisfied by reading. Also, I discovered I was something of an artist and spent lots of time drawing things that I saw in nature. Papa complained that he would go broke buying me art supplies. But let me tell you, anytime his Esther needed something for drawing, my Papa would make it magically appear in my drawing supplies box.

I loved school and I adored Mrs. Goldenberg, our school teacher. As she was also the religious school's teacher, she taught me about Judaism and how to read Hebrew. She and her husband were frequent visitors at our home on Sabbath. I was an excellent student and even entertained thoughts of college.

One day, when I was eighteen, my sister and I were out on a walk and suddenly we were confronted by two ruffians who had decided that they wanted see how the "Jew girls" looked without their shirts on.

The boys were much bigger than we were. I was scared and my little sister started crying. I was looking for a place to run, when I noticed Manny, the blacksmith's son, coming up behind them. He was easily a head shorter than either of the ruffians, about the same height as me. He was wide and appeared rather pudgy.

"You should leave them alone," Manny told them in a menacing tone.

They laughed at him and told him to go away. He walked right up to them and one of the boys threw a powerful blow into Manny's belly. It hurt me to watch, but Manny didn't even flinch.

In the blink of an eye, he had knocked their heads together. They fell to the ground but jumped up quickly. One of them grabbed a large stick and the other was using both hands to pick up a heavy paving stone. While the first ruffian swung the stick at Manny's face, the other was slowly coming up behind him holding the large rock over his head. While Manny caught the stick in his hand before it hit his face, I jumped at the boy with the stone and pulled on one of his arms. That caused the ruffian to lose control of the stone which then came down and hit him on the head. He tried to turn toward me, but the blow to his head made him stagger sideways and he collapsed to a sitting position on the ground.

When I looked back at Manny, he had the other boy over his head. Manny threw him onto his collapsed partner as easily as my father threw logs onto a fire. The ruffian who I hit in the head with his own rock staggered to his feet. He glared at me and yelled, "You!" He started running toward me. His forward progress was abruptly terminated by a lightening blow from Manny's fist into his face. He screamed in pain at what was probably a broken nose and at that point the two ruffians had enough and ran away.

Manny turned toward us and modestly said to me, "It's a good thing you helped me, or that guy could have killed me with that rock."

"No," I told him. "If it wasn't for you, this would have been a disaster for us. Those guys scared us and you saved us."

"I can walk you home if you want," Manny offered.

"I don't think those guys will bother us again, but maybe you should walk us home anyway," I replied.

As we walked home, Manny started telling me about the books he was reading that he borrowed from the school teacher, Mrs. Goldenberg. He said he was learning about material science and just loved it.

I asked why he wasn't in school and he told me that he had to help his father at the blacksmith shop. But his mother made an arrangement with his father some years before she died, that Manny would be allowed to read at least two hours a day and all day during Sabbath.

I told him that I loved art and drawing. He told me that he couldn't draw but that his favorite artist was Meindert Hobbema.

"He was a post-Renaissance Dutch artist who," Manny informed me, "lived in the 1600s. I particularly admire his woodland landscapes. I've never seen one of his paintings in person, but I saw his work in some of the books I borrowed."

At one point I tripped on some lose gravel and fell against him. It was like tumbling into a stone wall. He put one of his powerful arms around my waist to catch me before I fell further. Then he stood me up at once, as if nothing happened and we continued walking. Although he didn't have his arms wrapped around me and he was only touching me for a few seconds, my body was reacting as if he had both his arms wrapped solidly around me for the last hour. In my young mind, I knew this guy was going to protect me, no matter what came along.

At one point I stopped and pointed out a cloud formation that I thought would be fun to draw. I grabbed his arm to stop him so he could see it, and I felt as if I was holding onto steel—he had looked pudgy but he was solid as an anvil.

As we gazed at the cloud formation, my little sister complained that it was just a cloud and there were lots of clouds.

"Use your imagination when you look at them and you can see many things, if you try. Also look at the texture of the clouds. Some are solid and dark, while others are soft, and some are wispy," Manny instructed my sister.

Suddenly my sister was staring intently at the clouds as if she was seeing them in a new way. She started shouting out all the things she saw in them that she'd never seen before.

And I was staring at Manny, the blacksmith's son, because I was seeing him in a new way too. My mind was shouting out all the things I was seeing in him for the first time.

Who was this guy? I saw him at Sabbath services occasionally, but had never talked to him before. Every time he opened his mouth, something intelligent fell out, like pearls from an oyster.

My little sister had never listened to anyone, but a few words from this blacksmith's son and she was seeing images in clouds.

And the way he smiled when he looked at me—even now, thinking about the way he smiled at me, even after all these years—I could just melt.

We started walking again and I suddenly wanted to know so much more about the blacksmith's son. "Do you always notice clouds?" I asked him.

"Well not so often, but my mother insisted I pay attention to the natural world. She told me its beauty gives us peace of mind and reminds us to be thankful for the beauty God put in the world for us to enjoy. I know she's right, but personally I'd rather make a tool and put it to work."

"You had a wise mother."

"I hear you can draw," Manny told me. "That's special. I can see a tool in my mind and know how to make it but I can't draw anything."

"I'll make a drawing of clouds for you because you rescued us today."

"And I'll make a box for you to keep things in, because you prevented my head from getting dented by that rock," he said in that gentle laughing tone of his. We arrived at my house and I said good bye.

He glanced over his shoulder as he walked away. "Maybe I'll see you again."

"I'll look forward to that."

My little sister ran in the house ahead of me to tell our mother what happened. Upon entering the house, my mother approached me asking if I was all right.

"Shifrah and I are fine because Manny rescued us," I told my mom with a huge smile.

"Manny, the blacksmith's son?" my mother asked astonished. "I always thought he was such a dull boy. He doesn't go to school. He hardly says anything to anybody."

"I'm making a drawing for him because he rescued us," I told my mother. "And he's making some kind of a box for me because he thinks I helped him with those ruffians."

"You'll be lucky to get anything beyond horse shoes from that one," my mother declared laughingly.

"Momma, when he stood, firmly as a rock, between your two daughters and those foul ruffians, even those dullards were smart enough to know that he wouldn't let any harm come to us. I felt so safe once he was there—and he's smart, Momma. He was telling me about something called metallurgy and how he uses it to make stronger tools at his father's shop."

My mother thought for a moment and said, "Yes, I remember the school teacher said that he read nearly every book at the school and she was getting him books on metals from the University Library to read. Okay, so you'll give him a drawing and that will be that."

"No, Momma. That will not be that. I'm going to marry him."

"What? No! Marry a blacksmith's son? No," Momma declared. "You're educated. You're beautiful. You don't even know him. You will not waste yourself on the son of a lowly blacksmith."

Remember, this was in the days of arranged marriages. I was violating lots of community mores by deciding on my own whom I would marry.

"Talk nice about him, Momma," I dared to say. "He's going to be the father of your grandchildren."

Momma was horrified and raged at me. "Wait 'til your father gets home. He'll put a stop to this foolishness."

My father took me aside when he arrived. "What's this I'm hearing from your mother? Is it true?"

"Yes, Poppa, it's true. I know it in my heart that we should be together."

"Have you talked to him about this?"

"No but I will and—"

"Then you better hurry," my Poppa said, "because the story around town is that he and his father, Avram, bought a saw mill and forge in some tiny town in Washington State and they're leaving in a month. They'll move and you'll never hear from him. And that will be better for all concerned. Believe me."

My heart was pounding in my chest when I heard they were planning to leave town. I started working on Manny's drawing immediately and made plans to visit the blacksmith's shop.

Two days later, on my way home from school, I stopped by the blacksmith's shop with my completed drawing.

The shop was a messy place with the smell of the hot metal, charcoal, and cigar smoke permeating the air. Pieces of metal were scattered all over the floor. Manny's dad was short too. He wore a big leather apron and heavy boots and he had a cigar clenched between his tobacco-stained teeth. He had a big infectious grin and sparkling blue eyes.

He took the cigar out of his teeth and with a huge smile said, "So, this is who my son is getting *mishuga* over. How do I know he's crazy over you? For years I can't get my son to make anything out of wood. Metal. He only wants to know about making things out of metal. Suddenly, two days ago, he's making a beautiful chest out of oak and cherry wood, with a cedar lining, and a special spring on the hinges so it's easy to open and close the heavy lid. He spends so much time sanding it smooth, I tell him he's going to sand it down until there's nothing left. And you know what else? He gave up his reading time to work on this cedar chest for you. Little lady, I'll tell you something, he never *ever* gives up his reading time, but he did give up his reading time to make something for *you*."

Then he kind of looked me up and down and said, "He's telling me that you're kinder and more intelligent than you are beautiful. From what I'm looking at, that may not be possible. Tell me, little lady, is that possible?"

It must have been the heat from the forge, because I felt my face was getting warm.

"Manny said that I'm kind?"

"Turn around. Ask him yourself."

Manny stood in the doorway. He was covered in sweat and his powerful arms glistened in the sunlight. His face shone with joy. I felt a warm feeling come over me and we hadn't even said a word to each other yet.

"Hello. I have a drawing for you."

"And I have a cedar-lined chest for storing blankets for you."

The way he looked at me—he made me feel good just smiling at me.

"*Kinder*," Manny's father told us, "go in the house to look at the drawing. The cedar chest is in there as well. I have work to do out here, so you'll be out of my way."

We entered their small house. Manny looked at the drawing for a long time and thanked me. He told me it was a treasure, an absolute treasure.

He showed me the cedar-lined chest. The outside was so smooth and shiny it almost looked wet. And the lid was easy to lift with the springs he had installed with the hinge. It obviously took many hours to build. And he made it with such care. Such care for me. How could I be so lucky? I told him that it was the most carefully crafted cedar chest I had ever seen.

"Well, you saved me," he said.

"No, you saved me," I told him.

He laughed that deep sounding laugh of his. "Okay. Okay. We saved each other," Manny said with a huge grin.

"I heard that you and your father will be moving in a month," I blurted out.

"We've bought a lumber mill and forge shop from a man who's retiring. It's far away in the Pacific Northwest." He took my little hands in his big powerful ones, looked at me earnestly, and said, "I'll be able to make a comfortable living for us, and I promise you our children will never be hungry."

And that was his marriage proposal to me. I was so thrilled because I absolutely knew he felt the same way about me as I felt about him.

"What's this? You two making a *shidekh*?" Manny's dad said as he entered the house.

"Yes, we are making a match," I told him, still looking into Manny's eyes. "In fact, I told my parents two days ago that I was going to marry him." Except for Manny holding my hands, I don't know where I found the strength to talk that way to an adult.

"Then you two deserve each other, because two days ago my son told me that he was going to marry you."

I squeezed Manny's hands when I heard what he said.

"Pa, don't embarrass me."

"Embarrass nothing. I went to the school teacher, Mrs. Goldenberg, to find out about this little lady. She told me that you two are the brightest kids in this town. Also she told me, more importantly, the two of you might be the nicest kids in this town. She said that if you two thought you should be together, then I shouldn't get in the way. The way the two of you look at each other, I'd have to be crazy not to give you my blessing. I'm going to get cleaned up so I can go talk to your father. Manny, you should do the same and we'll go together."

I walked home alone worrying about my parents' reaction.

Manny and his father came over to our house that evening. My father had a talk with Manny's dad in the kitchen.

"I'm just a blacksmith, but my son is much more," I overheard Manny's father say. "We're not buying a business in Washington State with the money I make from horse shoes and wagon repairs—Manny's reading and understanding about metal brings ideas into my shop that let me make tools in an hour that used to take all day. Even the Amish come to my shop to buy, because they know our tools are stronger and will last longer. *Oy*! He has such a head that he makes tools that make tools. Do you understand this? A steel salesman from Chicago came through here last month. He and Manny are talking about carbon and hardness in vocabulary I've never heard. After talking to Manny for a couple of hours about the metal Manny needed, the salesman told me, 'He's a natural engineer, that one.' And the math he does. Equations, he calls them. Squiggles here, letters there, numbers over numbers—and suddenly my tools are stronger."

My momma came into the room at that point. "Well, what have you two decided for them?"

"I'm not sure," my father said.

"Well, get sure," my mother instructed him. "Because I'm sure now. I wasn't before, but do you hear that laughter? That's Shifrah and Moishe laughing at a story he's telling them about a funny creature that lives under a bridge. As he's telling the story to them, he's making them characters in the story. I think Esther should be so lucky to have a man that will entertain her children. And the way Esther looks at him, the only decision you two should make is when will be the wedding!"

"This is not an easy decision for a father to make," my poppa said.

My mother was quiet for a moment and then told him, "The most miserable time of my life was the weeks it took to travel here from Europe with the girls. I was nervous, anxious, and sick from the sea. But the minute I left the train and saw you smiling at me, all the pain of the trip was gone and I knew I was home and safe. That's how she looks at him."

My father smiled at my mother, then as he shook the black-smith's hand he said, "So now we'll see when the Rabbi can come to town."

A week later, as the Rabbi descended from the train, my father greeted him and said, "We are glad you arrived here so quickly."

He replied in a laughter filled voice, "So I get this message from a teacher, a Mrs. Goldenberg, who says that two of her best students need a rabbi down here, like yesterday. I told her that I wasn't sure about my schedule. She gets mad and tells me that if I don't show up and marry these two, she'll fix it so I can never borrow another book from any library in the state for the rest of my life. I know a real threat when I hear one so I boarded the next train."

We had a wonderful wedding ceremony. My mother made a beautiful *Chuppa* for us and Manny's dad made a lovely support for it. We stood on a little raised platform during the ceremony. At the end, when the groom breaks a glass under his foot to remind us of the destruction of the temple in Jerusalem—Manny being Manny, not only smashed the glass under his foot, but also jammed his foot through one of the boards we were standing on. He was embarrassed, but we all laughed.

We shipped all our goods out ahead of us to Washington State. We said our tearful good-byes and boarded the train to start our new life in the Northwest. As the train pulled out of the station I never knew if I would see any of my brothers and sisters again.

• • • •

I FELT QUITE SAD TO leave my family behind in Iowa. My parents were sad that I was going so far away, but understood that my future was with Manny. My sister, Shifrah, however, wasn't ready to lose her big sister and it was difficult for her to watch me leave. I promised I would write to her regularly.

My wedding night with Manny was difficult, to say the least. It was August in Iowa and humid—like you were dressed in a warm, damp sponge. Well, neither of us knew anything about sex. We had the general idea from watching farm animals that his thing had to go in my thing, but not much else. As far as advice from my mother, all she'd told me was sex is this awful thing you have to do with men if you want to have kids and keep the man happy.

We were both sweating profusely, Manny was pushing, and I was in pain and wondering why it hurt so much. The moment I started to feel a little pleasure, Manny made some noises, I felt his thing moving inside me, and it was over. He rolled off me and went to sleep. Not exactly something I would be looking forward to doing again.

We boarded the train that took us to Minneapolis as the first part of our journey. The smells, smoke, and noise from the steam engine were dreadful. By mid-day we were covered in oily soot and smelled liked burned coal. Every now and then the train would be on a curve and the smoke poured in the windows. People tried to quickly close them, but at least some of the smoke would get in the train car. It was terrible. It was much better when we were traveling across the northern plains as the temperatures cooled off to a reasonable degree, especially at night—the seats transformed into beds then, and had curtains surrounding them for privacy.

Manny's father found some men his age at the back of our train and they played cards all the way to Seattle.

On the afternoon of the first day on the train, Manny was at the rear of our car talking to his dad and a middle-aged woman sat down next to me and we talked.

She introduced herself as Rose Mendoza. She was dressed fashionably and had a rather *zaftig* figure. Rose was excited to meet a fellow Jew who was moving to the Seattle area. When she realized I was a newlywed, she was excited for me. She was even more excited to learn that we were going to be living near her. We talked about many topics—she was obviously a well-read woman.

"Your husband is a nice looking man. He looks so strong," Rose told me. She looked around for a moment and then lowered her voice to a whisper. "Honey, how was your first night with him?"

I was shocked that she would ask me about that. To the best of my memory, I don't remember anyone, other than my mother, talking to me about sex.

I must have worn that shock on my face, because Rose continued, "The answer should have been that it was the most incredible thing ever. Seeing that you have that shocked look on your face, instead of a huge smile, we need to talk. First of all, he needs to go slow before he even gets inside you. And once he's inside you, he waits until you finish first. Then he can finish. And when he's done, he holds you. You tell him that and you'll be surprised how much you will enjoy it. Now, when he does it right, you tell him how much of a man he is and how great he makes you feel, and he'll do anything to keep you saying that. It won't be long before your body starts telling you that you want him, as much as he wants you. Sometimes he'll think he's too tired to do something, but you just get your hands on his business down there and he'll do anything you want him to, tired or not."

Well I was sure my jaw had dropped all the way to the floor of the train.

"Look—my Harry is coming this way," she whispered to me in an excited tone.

Harry, a fashionably dressed but otherwise unremarkable-looking man, walked up, smiled at Rose, bent over, and kissed his wife on the cheek, then continued on his way.

"See that," Rose had a big grin on her face, "twenty-two years together and he still makes me feel glad that I'm a woman. You talk to your Manny. You'll see. He'll make you feel that way too."

My mind was spinning. Unlike my mother, this woman looked forward to the bedtime business. Our conversation continued about things I could expect in my new Northwest home, plus discussions on education and job training. We exchanged addresses and Rose told me to send her a note when we were settled. She'd promised me, "I'll teach you how to make salmon gefilte fish. Plus many of the Jews up in the Northwest are *Sephardi*. Harry's mother taught me lots of *Sephardi* recipes and we'll get together and have fun baking and cooking for the holidays."

I liked this outspoken lady. I remember thinking that I hoped we would become friends, even though she was much older than I was.

That night, I talked to Manny as Rose had suggested. It took us a couple of tries, but the last night on the train I, you know, finished. Manny tried to hold me afterward, but I kept kissing him and rubbing my body against him because he made me feel so great. I think my legs must have been brushing against his business, because I realized he was ready to do it again and, yes, I finished again too. Married life was improving by the moment for Manny and me.

As we were leaving the train I said good-bye to Harry and Rose. "I hope to see you again," I told them.

"You will, dear," Rose told me. Then she whispered, "So, did he take you there?"

I could feel my face turning red, but I leaned toward her, lowered my voice to a whisper and said, "Twice."

"I told you," she whispered in a high-pitched voice. "He's a good man, just like my Harry."

Then they turned and walked away, arm in arm—two unremarkable-looking people who shared a most remarkable love. It really inspired me to see that love really can last a lifetime.

Well, the first day in our new home, I mostly spent cleaning and putting things away, but then, just before dinner, a messenger arrived with a box addressed to Manny and me. I opened it and found two jars of canned fruit I never heard of, a *mezuzah*, a spice cake, and a dinner invitation for Saturday night. It was from Rose and Harry, of course.

The invitation said she was inviting some of her friends from ORT she wanted me to meet. I didn't know it then, but the local ORT chapter didn't make a move without consulting Rose. When there was a conflict, she would gather the parties in conflict over tea and spice cake at her home. A resolution would appear as quickly as her spice cake disappeared. I sent a message, accepting her invitation, back with the messenger. Rose and I became lifelong friends.

As we were moving into our new home, the local priest stopped by. He was a fit-looking man of average height. His demeanor was one of jolly confidence.

"Good day, Mr. and Mrs. Weiss. I'm Father O'Malley from St. Bridget's, up the street there," he gestured in that direction, "across from what I hear is your new business. Welcome to town. I'm glad to hear that we have more members of the Hebrew faith moving in. Won't be long and I'll bet we'll all be pitching in to help build a synagogue."

This was followed by a thunderous laugh. He shook our hands and saw my Sabbath candleholders that I had brought from Iowa.

"And do you light candles on the beginning of your Sabbath each Friday?" he asked.

"Always," I replied. "We do a little service and discuss a portion of the bible, as well."

"It's been quite some time since I attended a Sabbath dinner," he told us with a twinkle in his eye.

"It would be an honor if you would like to join us this Friday," I told him. "We'll begin at seven o'clock."

"I'll be here," he replied.

"By the way, Mr. Weiss, if you need to hire a few lads, let me know. I know of a few good fellas that have been looking for work.

Manny thanked him. "That's good to know, Father O'Malley."

And so our first Sabbath guest was a priest. As wonderful a man as you would ever want to meet. He shocked us when he arrived with a box of kosher Sabbath candles for me. What an amazingly thoughtful gift. We were happy to get to know him.

The following afternoon Manny, Avram, and I traveled over to Rose and Harry's home. They lived in a two-story house with a wide front porch. The house was surrounded by a short picket fence and the landscaping was neat and orderly. At the side of the front door was a sign that read Harry Mendoza, MD.

We saw Harry seated in a rocking chair reading a newspaper. As we opened the gate to the yard, Harry saw us and yelled into the screened front door, "They're here, Rose!" Harry opened the door for us and whispered, "She's been cooking all day. You better be hungry."

"That won't be a problem for this group," I told him.

"Welcome, welcome," Rose told us as she came out of the kitchen smiling broadly and wiping her hands on her flour-covered apron. She took off the apron and had hugs for everyone—her bright and bubbly spirit made us feel at home right away.

"Dinner is almost ready, so let's sit down and Harry will pour us some wine."

The table was set with lovely dishes. I was seated next to Rose with Manny next to me and Avram seated across the table from us. Rose and I had table settings that were much more intricately patterned than the settings for the men.

"Harry bought these for me when he was in Sheffield, England and I always put them out for my lady friends," she explained.

Dinner started with chicken soup and salad with a light dressing. The main course consisted of poached salmon filet, a *Sephardic*-style casserole of lamb and apricots seasoned with honey, coriander and ginger, a spinach soufflé, plus lamb and vegetable-stuffed red onions.

"I didn't have enough dried apricots so I added some dried nectarines as well."

After explaining my ignorance of nectarines, Harry told me, "Nectarines are a type of peach and they grow on peach trees, but don't have the fuzzy skin. I have some fruit trees growing behind the house that provide us peaches and nectarines every year. Rose dries some and cans the rest. The trees are blooming now, so it won't be many more weeks until we have fresh peaches and nectarines."

I heard that the Northwest was famous for apples so I asked if they grew them as well.

"Apples," Rose exclaimed. "Esther, we get apples around here like crazy. They're easy to grow, but they also come out of the valley east of here near a town called, Yakima. They come in various shades of green, yellow, and red. Some are as sweet as honey and others sour and firm—which are perfect for baking and cooking. You'll be amazed at how many different types of apples will be available and the thousands of ways you can add them to dishes."

She also told me about the raspberries that grew wild all over the area. And cherries which, like the raspberries, I had to admit I read about, but never eaten.

Dessert took care of that. Rose served raspberry cobbler, cherry pie, and a tort made with dried apples and walnuts seasoned with molasses, nutmeg, and cinnamon.

Manny leaned over and whispered to me, "It looks like we'll be eating well in the Northwest."

Rose, naturally, wrote down all the recipes for me. I was amazed at the range of flavors in the dishes she served. We talked cooking, gardening, and housekeeping, especially those things that were different here in the Northwest as opposed to Iowa.

After dinner, some of Rose's friends from ORT came over and we drank tea together. They explained their charity work in the hope I would find time to join and help their group. They were raising money to send to schools, for Jews who would be coming to the United States. The students needed job skills they could put to immediate use when they arrived here.

"Many of them only know life on the farm, but need to understand how to work with machinery when they get here," Rose informed me.

What could be better than helping people learn job skills so they could take care of themselves? This was a wonderful idea, and I told them that they could count on me to help.

"I'm so glad you feel that way," Rose said.

As they discussed various upcoming projects, I let them know what I would like to do. One of the projects consisted of setting up an English-language library so students could read about the US and its constitution. I immediately volunteered to run that project knowing I would write a letter to Mrs. Goldenberg back in Iowa for recommendations of books we should purchase for the library.

Rose was glowing when I volunteered. This was obviously an organization of doers, not talkers. Certainly, this was my type of group.

Traveling home, I told Manny about ORT and what help I offered.

Manny told me, "Harry said he and some other doctors want to build a hospital closer to our town. I'm going to meet with him, and some of the other business owners in the area, to discuss plans."

Then Avram told us, "We've barely been here a week and I feel like I have known these people all my life. I'm sure I'll get to know Harry well. After all, he's a card player."

We all laughed. Avram was right. He and Harry became best friends. In between card games, Harry showed Avram how to plant and prune fruit trees for our yard. The two of them were practically inseparable in the spring, summer, and fall, helping each other with their orchards. Avram started reading about trees and how to take care of them. Within a few years people from all over our town were coming by to ask Avram or Harry about taking care of their fruit trees.

On one of his trips to the University in Seattle to learn more about metallurgy, Manny met a university professor that taught classes in arboriculture. He arranged for a private class for Avram and Harry. The professor took the train to our town and spent an entire weekend talking trees and tree cultivation.

Avram and Harry were like school children. The professor even lent them some books from the university library to study. Within weeks, the two of them memorized the books and sent them back to the professor. One of my strongest memories of that time was watching Avram sitting with a text book, a note book, and a dictionary. Whatever he lacked in brain power, he made up for in effort.

The two men had an interesting effect on each other. Avram taught Harry how to relax, which included daily walks. And Avram started reading the newspaper every day, as well as getting books from the library so he could become more knowledgeable about the subjects that he and Harry discussed during their walks.

Prior to their friendship, apparently no one could convince Harry to relax. All he thought about was his Rose, his children, and his medical practice. Not necessarily in that order. Rose tried to get him to relax for years. Nothing doing. Not until Avram came along.

It started when Avram kept asking Harry to walk with him. Finally, Harry agreed on the condition Avram would give up smoking on their walking days.

After a few weeks of giving up those foul cigars, Avram started feeling better than he had in years—he gave up smoking completely.

As for Harry, the walks demonstrated what terrible shape he was in; after a few blocks he was out of breath. "I'm going to start walking every day, Rose," he told his wife. "What kind of an example do I represent for my patients when I can't even walk far with my friend, Avram?"

And so, the two men could be seen on daily walks, rain or shine, every afternoon with the only exceptions being for medical emergencies.

Rose mentioned to me that Harry told her, "It's those walks and those fruit trees, you know. I get such a contented feeling when Avram and I are out walking around town or working on those trees. It's not like relaxing doing nothing, but I enjoy it so."

Avram was also thrilled with his new friendship. "Who would have thought—a doctor and a blacksmith? What a wonderful friend I have," he told me.

Manny's business was a challenge at first. The machines were put on the floor without any thought of work flow. After each machine did its job, men would hand carry the pieces to the next machine. The floor was filthy with scrap wood, shavings, and sawdust lying around everywhere. There was one small, filthy toilet for the men to use at the back of the shop. The walls hadn't been cleaned in years and there was an obvious bearing problem in at least two of the machines. It took many months to improve.

Manny's strength and mind soon found the way to success—and we all knew how strong my Manny was, but the following month I found he was powerful in another way. I was pregnant.

Chapter Ten ~ Lessons Learned from Children

WITH ALL HER WONDERFUL stories, we convinced Grandma Esther to come live with us.

Her main concern was that she would be a burden to us so we eventually agreed she could pay us rent. She would have her own apartment at our house with its own entrance.

Esther flew back to Iowa and I arranged for a moving company to pack all her things and ship them to our home. Before her things arrived, we received a large crate. Joan and I opened it with curiosity and found the cedar chest Manny made for Esther.

It had beautiful Pendleton blankets inside it, both new designs and old. We also found a hand-written note inside the chest that read:

Kinder,
I hope the blankets you place inside this old chest will bring warmth to your lives like your Grandfather Manny brought to mine.
Love,
Grandma Esther

The chest was still in great condition. The finish had worn in a few places and one of the hinges which held the lid open needed repair. It was easy to lightly sand the exterior and put a modern finish on the outside so it would last another sixty-plus years. I also wound a new spring for the hinge so it worked like new. The interior cedar boards needed slight sanding and the chest was as good as new.

It fit into our home as easily as Esther did. She joined us when she wanted and stayed in her apartment when she wanted. She and Samantha developed an especially close relationship. They went for walks together, read together, and baked together.

Joan became pregnant six months after our wedding, and if it was possible, Esther was happier than ever thinking about, and planning for, a new baby in the house.

Great-Grandma Esther was absolutely walking on air, thinking about the baby. I was so relieved that she would be here for Joan during that time, especially since Joan's mom was gone.

Joan's sister, Golda was nearly as happy as Joan—both she and Aaron had been with Joan during the dark days of her mastectomy and were overjoyed to find out Joan was able to have more children.

I imagined Esther spending her days reading and taking it easy after she moved in. Wrong! As soon as she was settled in her apartment, she called up the local ORT chapter and told them she was back in town. The daughter of an old friend of hers, the woman Rose she had told us about, drove over the next day to pick Esther up to attend a luncheon and meet more of the local ORT members.

Now, Esther has different groups of ORT members in her apartment a few times a month. One time she was telling us she had to head to her apartment and make a spice cake for the women who were coming over. I offered to run to the local bakery to get something for her so she wouldn't have to bake.

She looked at me as if I was crazy and said, "Only if they make spice cake using Rose Mendoza's recipe."

I don't know why that was funny, but Esther sure did.

We'd been trying to involve Samantha in getting ready for the baby as much as possible too. She'd been having a difficult time understanding the new baby would be a boy. When we went to the children's furniture store, she kept picking out items more suitable for a girl. Joan kept trying to explain to her she should be looking for things a boy would enjoy.

Hands on hips she explained, "Mom, I have a tough time talking to boys. I sure don't know what they want."

"What do you think your dad would want?" Joan asked her.

"Come on, Mom! He's going to be too small to drive a boat or something from Dad's car collection—and unless he's like Nathan, he won't care much about math for a lot of years."

When we asked Samantha how she could help her brother become part of the family, she told us, "I can help him by telling him he has a strict dad and mom."

Nine months later, Ari Minkowski entered our lives, and Samantha had been right about one thing, Ari wouldn't have Nathan's interest in math, but things with engines—don't ask!

Once Ari came home, he never lacked for attention. Between Esther, Joan, Samantha, his Uncle Aaron, his Aunt Golda, my cousin Dov, and his wife Cora, some of the family were wondering if the first words he would say were going to be, "Put me down!"

One Saturday morning, Joan was seated on the deck overlooking the lake outside our bedroom. Ari was around ten-months-old, and she was holding him in a standing position on her lap when a seaplane with an old radial engine flew slowly down the lake. As its rumbling sound passed in front of them, Joan noticed Ari turned his head toward the sound and his eyes followed the plane as it cruised down the lake.

She started watching when loud boats raced past. Ari always stopped what he was doing to look for the source of the sound. In fact, Joan claimed that Ari was imitating engine noises before he started talking and "motor" was his first actual word.

Joan noted that, as a preschooler, Ari's favorite time was when I would take him for a ride in one of my antique cars. He especially enjoyed a noisy ride in my shiny black Superformance GT40. Joan was convinced that the black GT40 was the first love in Ari's life.

Ari was single minded. He did what he wanted to do and no amount of explanation would deter him. This was most frustrating to Joan, but less so for me. For example, I warned a three-year-old Ari that he should stay away from the street because he might get hurt.

The next day Ari came up, stood in front of me with his little hands on his hips, and angrily told me, "I went near the street and I didn't get hurt."

"Oh yes you did," I yelled, grabbing Ari on the back of his collar with my left hand and giving him a quick slap on his bottom with my right.

Ari learned quickly that it wasn't a good idea to upset me, because there might be hell to pay. But he knew he could get away with more when Joan was involved, because that generally meant a lecture, after which he could go back to doing what he wanted. It wasn't long before he found that he could debate with his mom during the lectures in order to extend the time before he had to start doing some household chore.

When he tried to argue with me, I would tell him, "Do what I tell you first, then we can discuss why."

Naturally that defeated the purpose Ari had in mind—putting off when he had to start doing some chore.

I eventually would get tired of hearing Joan and Ari arguing and would tell him in a stern tone, "I don't want to hear anymore debating between you and your mother. When she tells you to do something, you do it first and you can debate about it after the task is done to your mother's satisfaction. Is that clear?"

"Yes, Dad," a thoroughly chastened Ari would reply.

When Ari went to school he didn't have many friends, mostly because few of his classmates shared his interest in things with engines, and none of them had his knowledge of them.

Samantha loved school and everyone wanted to be her friend. All her teachers loved her too. Even the teachers she didn't enjoy weren't aware she didn't like them.

Ari started reading during his fourth year and read anything to do with engines. Appropriately, the first pure fiction book he read occurred in second grade and was titled, *The Red MG*. He wasn't much of a student and was generally bored in class. Oddly enough, by fourth grade he became a voracious reader who also liked historical fiction. His latest read was *Exodus*.

Joan and I were called in by Ari's fourth grade teacher, "When we do arts and crafts projects, Ari does them poorly and tries to finish them as quickly as possible, without putting any effort into them."

Joan saw I was getting angry and she put her hand on my arm to signal to me to calm down.

I glanced at Joan with what I'm sure was an annoyed look on my face then said to the teacher, "I think cutting and pasting are a waste of time for fourth graders. Do you have any idea what level of reading Ari is at?"

"He does well on spelling tests and his reading skills are adequate, but he doesn't seem to show any interest in the stories we have in class."

"Adequate? Adequate?" I said as my blood began to boil. My voice was getting louder as I became angrier.

"I brought one of the books he's currently reading at home. It's *The Tell*, by Leon Uris. He just finished reading *Exodus*. The next book he's asked for is *Chesapeake*, by Michener. If you're his teacher, why didn't you know that he was way ahead of most of his classmates?"

"I'm certainly aware of his reading skills."

"Then tell me which of your other students are reading the same books as Ari," I demanded.

The teacher was getting flustered and tried to regain control of the situation, "I think this misses the point—"

I cut her off. "No, that *is* the point. You are boring the hell out of my son, and I suspect that's true for many of his fellow students. If you don't like what I'm saying, then we can head over to the principal's office and discuss it with him. I am furious that my tax money isn't educating my son."

"I don't think that will be necessary, Mr. Minkowski. I just wanted to make sure you were aware of Ari's shortcomings, as far as his school work is concerned."

"I want to assure you, you have certainly informed me of the shortcomings around here."

As Joan and I walked out to the car, she could see I was about to explode. "Okay, you're right," she told me, clearly trying to head off an argument. "We should have put him in private school to begin with. They don't have a clue what to do with exceptional children at some schools. I'll start looking into private schools as soon as we get home."

As it turns out, private school was perfect for Ari. After being there for a few weeks, one of the school counselors called Joan and suggested Ari should be tested for Attention Deficit Disorder. Joan talked to our children's pediatrician who said we should try a medication that would either make a huge difference or not do anything. Fortunately for Ari, it worked. His grades shot up in all his classes.

This had an additional effect. As the pediatrician was describing the symptoms of ADD, Joan realized that was exactly what I experienced. So, she managed to set aside a few of Ari's pills for me to try. Not only could I concentrate on subjects other than mathematics, but my mood swings disappeared. I went to my own general practitioner for a prescription for the same medication. I learned from my doctor most people with ADD self-select a career that accommodates their ADD.

"In fact," he told me, "more ER docs have ADD than they would care to admit."

I regularly thanked the Lord for that medication, as did Joan who found living with me much improved. When she saw me getting angry, she started asking if I took my medication that day, at which point I looked at her, either telling her no and calming down, or giving her a dirty look because I *had* taken the medication and was still angry. This would sometimes be followed by a verbal explosion on my part, while Joan would try to calm me down.

I often called Joan my emotional thermometer, as she would try to take over the situation to remove me from the environment that was causing me to get angry. Interesting enough, Ari also developed this skill as he became older.

He would tell me, "You're getting angry, Dad."

More often than not, this would surprise me, as I wasn't even aware I was getting angry. I usually calmed down when Ari told me that.

This surprised my father. "You listen to him?"

"Why shouldn't I listen to him? He's almost always right."

• • • •

ESTHER AND SAMANTHA were spending Saturday mornings together each week while Ari, Joan, and I walked over to my cousin, Rabbi Dov's house for Torah study. Each week we reviewed part of the Torah and the commentary various Rabbis have written concerning that section of the Hebrew Bible.

One Saturday, when Jonathan was eleven, Dov had just concluded the session for the day and was telling us the reading in one week was fascinating because of the commentary by the great scholar Rashi. Jonathan became quite agitated at this point—it was difficult enough to understand him when he was calm, but when he was excited it was particularly challenging. Dov looked at Nathan, who was better at understanding what Jonathan was saying when he became excited.

"He said the commentary you are referring to is at least four weeks away and not next week." Nathan told us.

One of the group members was bent over at his desk, looking to verify what Jonathan said. With a huge smile on his face, he sat up straight and said, "He's right, Rabbi! He's Right!"

"Pardon me, everyone, fortunately for us, my son, Jonathon, has corrected me," Dov said with obvious pride. "Looks like I have a real Torah *Bocher* in my house."

Dov called his wife, Cora, to come over and learn what Jonathan had accomplished. Naturally, she was beaming when she heard.

"See? What do I always tell you?" She said smiling at Jonathan. "Look what you've contributed today."

Torah stories fascinated Jonathan since he was little and when we thought he was just sitting and doing nothing in his wheelchair, he was thinking about those stories, and especially the commentary he'd heard about them.

"Especially Rashi's commentary," he said.

Samantha and Grandma Esther came over to Dov and Cora's house as the study group was ending. Our family members gathered for lunch. Did I tell you that Cora was a wonderful cook? Let me tell you, she can cook. She served blueberry blintzes, spinach soufflé, smoked white fish, French toast made from leftover *Challah*, plus a tray of lox, bagels, and cream cheese.

As I sat down, Joan sent me that *eat-slow* look she sends me when it appears like I am going to inhale a meal instead of eat it.

I told Samantha what Jonathan had done in the study group.

"I know. He knows all the Torah. Remember when I drew a picture of Noah and the Ark a few weeks ago? Jonathan told me the story and what lessons I could learn from it. Whenever we get together, he tells me another Torah story and its lessons.

"Wait until he tells you the story about the burning bush. It was on fire but not being burned up. He explains stories so well I told him he should write a children's book about the Torah."

We parents were shocked to hear about all this. I always wondered what Samantha and Jonathan spent so much time talking about, but foolishly assumed it was child talk. I never thought he was teaching her Torah.

"Jonathan can't write," Joan explained to Samantha.

"So he can tell me and I'll write them," Samantha announced.

Cora suggested, "Samantha, I'll tell you what. I'll write down the stories if you would draw the illustrations for them. If you have trouble, your mom can help you. What do you say?"

"That would be fun," an elated Samantha exclaimed.

Over the next year my six-year-old daughter spent many hours with her mom working on illustrations. Joan would read a new section of Jonathan's book to Samantha and they would discuss what an appropriate illustration would look like. Samantha would plunge into a drawing with occasional advice from her mom. It was becoming obvious that Samantha was an industrious worker who kept on task through completion. That first book was published just prior to Jonathan's *Bar Mitzvah*.

• • • •

WHEN WE GATHERED FOR Jonathan's *Bar Mitzvah*, there was a feeling of immense pride in the family for Jonathan's accomplishments. His preparation for his *Bar Mitzvah* and his knowledge of Torah were superb. The glow from his parent's expressions could have illuminated an entire city at midnight.

Before reading Jonathan's *Bar Mitzvah* speech to the congregation, the Rabbi commented on Jonathan's work ethic and love of Torah. He had memorized and analyzed a tremendous amount of Torah and Torah commentary.

The beginning of Jonathan's speech analyzed the day's *Parsha* from a number of viewpoints and what each of us could learn from it to improve our lives. Near the end, Jonathan thanked his parents and family for all their help and their continual belief in his ability to get things done.

"Not like there was a choice in my house," the Rabbi continued reading to us. "My parents never allowed me to feel sorry for myself.

In fact, they never let me have *time* to feel sorry for myself. They expect the same level of commitment to my tasks as they do of my brother, Nathan. And that's a lot, isn't it, Nathan? Once my mom and dad realized how quickly I could memorize Torah, they told me this was a gift from God and I had a responsibility to use that gift. Of course, that just meant I had to work harder to learn much more. Thanks to all my friends and family for their patience with my speech and physical disabilities. I know it is difficult to understand me, especially when I get excited. Right, Dad? Thanks to all the doctors, plus the speech and physical therapists, who did so much to help me over the years, so I am able to do many more things to take care of myself than I could a few years ago. Thanks to my brother, Nathan, who never complained when I took so much of our parents' attention to address my disabilities—and who still tries to teach me the mathematics that brings him so much joy. I'm sorry, Nathan. I get joy watching you get excited about your mathematics, but your calculus equations might as well be written in Chinese."

The Rabbi smiled as he read. "The other day Nathan was telling me about a transfer equation. Did you know there were equations that could transfer something? Who knew? When I was younger and feeling sad about my lack of abilities, my mother would tell me, 'At a minimum you can be an example to your younger brother of how to be a good person.' I have to admit there were many times when my brother was a good example for me. Thank you for being such a great brother, Nathan."

Nathan beamed with happiness.

Jonathan looked pleased as the Rabbi continued to read. "It was my father who always reminded me that while my body was in a wheelchair, my mind wasn't. Naturally, this was followed with, 'So get busy and study'. A special thank you goes to my cousin Samantha, who has incredible patience when listening to me. It was her idea I become the author of a children's book about Torah. She always has time to discuss the week's *Parsha* with me. I'm proud to say that she is the illustrator—with Aunt Joan's assistance—of my first book. Most of all, thanks to my parents who pushed, prodded, and poked, both my body and my mind to always do my best and be the best person I could be. With family like this surrounding me, I know I'll be able to live a Torah and joy filled life."

The Rabbi gestured toward Jonathan, indicating he was done reading and everyone cheered for Jonathan. We were all so very proud of him and what he had accomplished. Jonathan was a living example of why we should not judge a book by its cover.

• • • •

A FEW YEARS LATER, Joan approached Samantha and told her she needed to start thinking about a project for her *Bat Mitzvah*.

So, Samantha started thinking about the kind of *Mitzvah* projects her older cousins completed. Jonathan had decided to give the proceeds from his first book to a charity for handicapped children in Israel. Nathan had volunteered to tutor students in learning Hebrew.

Samantha decided to go to Great-Grandma Esther to discuss her ideas. She'd told her she wanted to do something to get children out of wheelchairs, and together they decided Samantha's *Mitzvah* project would need a great name, so they called it Kids Don't Belong in Wheelchairs.

Great-Grandma Esther helped her identify four charities performing research on neuromuscular diseases that would be equal beneficiaries of her fundraising project. To get her project off the ground, Joan and Samantha made some posters and Great-Grandma Esther brought Samantha to a gathering of her friends to make a presentation about her project.

She'd received her first checks that day, and some of the women gave her the work phone numbers of their husbands and told her to call and make an appointment to tell them about her *Bat Mitzvah* project.

Samantha rehearsed a speech, and Joan or I would drive her and her posters around to tell people about the project. All the husbands of the women who'd heard Samantha's presentation the first time had checks they presented to her as well.

One time, she'd visited a small stationary store where she'd pitched her project—they not only gave her a check, but printed beautiful thank-you notes for her to use.

A few months before her *Bat Mitzvah*, Samantha was studying with our congregation's Rabbi and he told her she was doing well in her studies for her *Bat Mitzvah*. He wanted to talk to her about a *Mitzvah* project. "Many of my students are volunteering at senior citizens homes," he said to her, "or volunteering to help tutor younger students learning Hebrew, or even volunteering at hospitals. What would you like to do?"

She proudly told him, "I already have a project. It's called Kids Don't Belong in Wheelchairs. I started working on it a year ago. The idea is to motivate companies and individuals to donate money to be divided between the four charities I have identified who are doing research on neuromuscular diseases."

"Samantha, I don't know if fundraising is an appropriate project. I think volunteering your time, working one-on-one with a needy person, is a better way to learn about *Tzedakah*."

In true Samantha fashion she replied, "I'm sorry Rabbi, but with all due respect, I think getting children out of wheelchairs is much more important. I have a cousin who has spent his entire life in a wheelchair. I could ask him if he'd rather spend time with me or have me spending time to get him out of the wheelchair, but I'm sure I know what his answer would be. Besides, this weekend my family and I are flying down to Florida to visit my dad's college roommate and pitch him on my project. I wasn't supposed to know, but I heard my dad tell my mom that he's giving me a check for ten thousand dollars."

"Ten thousand dollars?" the Rabbi asked incredulously.

"Yes." Samantha swelled with pride. "I have twenty-three thousand dollars in the bank now and if I get to fifty thousand, some of the people who have already given me donations will give me an extra five thousand dollars. My grandmother even had me describe my project to a large group of her friends. I think this is a great *Mitzvah* project."

"Well, Samantha, I have to agree with you," the Rabbi conceded. "We must remember this when you are older. We have a fundraising committee here at the synagogue and they could use someone like you."

Samantha chose a fascinating *Parsha* to discuss at her *Bat Mitzvah*, and naturally, Jonathan helped her analyse it. After more than a year of study preparing for her *Bat Mitzvah*, it was Samantha's chance to be the center of attention in our family for a weekend. And let me tell you, she was excited.

Time flies, and just a few years later, we would be gathering for Ari's *Bar Mitzvah*.

Chapter Eleven ~ Ari's Bar Mitzvah Week

MY COLLEGE ROOMMATE, Larry, and his wife, Danielle, came out for the entire week of Ari's *Bar Mitzvah*. They brought their children, Austin, Ann, Marsha, and Leah along as well. Leah is the youngest, born a month after Ari. We planned to go to Florida for Leah's *Bat Mitzvah* the following month. Everyone was excited to see each other again.

It was a blessing for the two families that Larry and I had stayed in touch after college. The families gathered at least once a year after Joan and I were married—sometimes twice a year. They were more like family than friends, and Joan and Danielle developed a close friendship. Samantha loved talking to Danielle about ethics. Samantha, Ann, and Leah became close and had lots of talks about girl stuff. Larry loved talking to Samantha and Ari, and I also spent many happy hours talking with Austin, Ann, and Marsha.

Marsha was a sweet child who appeared to get along with everyone, but never seemed really close to anyone. Instead of giving her own opinion, Marsha seemed to tell the listener what she thought they wanted to hear. Even Larry said once that he didn't know how Marsha felt about anything.

The older she became, the more distant she became. Danielle told us Marsha talked with her about how a person knows right from wrong when most children her age would be playing with friends—Marsha had few of those.

She took many long walks by herself, even though Larry and Danielle often tried to get her involved in art, music, sports, and dance. Nothing seemed to interest her. They'd told us she started seeing a therapist on an occasional basis around nine years of age.

The winter before Samantha's *Bat Mitzvah*, we'd gathered together with Larry and Danielle's family for a vacation at Disneyworld. Ari and Leah were about seven-years-old and they were immediately attracted to each other. They went on most of the rides together. At times I thought they were oblivious to the rest of us. They were the only seven-year-olds, so it seemed quite natural that they would want to be together.

Occasionally they both wanted to do something no one else wanted to do; they were too young to go alone so Samantha volunteered to go with them. I didn't realize it until years later, but Samantha was the first one in the family to treat them like a little couple. I don't know how she sensed it, but she did.

Once Samantha developed an idea of what they thought was fun, she would look for activities they could enjoy together. Needless to say, they adored Samantha. Leah and Ari screamed together on the children's roller coaster rides, shot water cannons at pretend enemies, laughed and joked with each other on train rides—all under Samantha's watchful eye.

I was amazed at Samantha's maturity in guiding the two of them. When they would argue about which activity to do next, Samantha would help them figure it out—she didn't decide for them, but helped them decide for themselves. She even chided them if their arguing became too loud. They would calm down immediately. No way were they going to disappoint Samantha.

At the end of that magical day we were all exhausted. Samantha, Leah, and Ari moved into the back seat of Larry's van. Samantha sat in the middle and seconds after Leah and Ari had their seat belts fastened, they were fast asleep, each of them leaning against Ari's big sister, who had her arms around them.

There was one constant whenever the families were together—within a couple of hours Ari and Leah would find activities they could do together. The older they became, the more they laughed, and the more they looked forward to seeing each other. Certainly as they grew older, they grew closer.

• • • •

SHORTLY AFTER LARRY'S family arrived at our home for Ari's *Bar Mitzvah*, I saw Ari walking up from our dock on the lake. A smiling Leah walked out to meet him and he started smiling too as soon as he spotted her. Ari was becoming a muscular thirteen-year-old, running daily and working out with weights at least three times a week. He also had a great tan. Joan sometimes referred to him as her little Greek god and always said he would be a real heartbreaker someday.

Leah was petite like her mom and inherited her mom's attractive good looks. Her dark hair was cut short. They walked up to each other and engaged in a brief hug.

We couldn't hear their words but their body language had clearly taken on a flirtatious tone since the last time our families were together.

Ari flexed a bicep and Leah gave him a playful push. He grinned at her and lifted up his t-shirt to show her his thirteen-year-old six-pack.

She shoved him again and they both laughed. They engaged in another longer hug and proceeded up to the house.

Joan and I looked at each other. "Were we doing that at their age?" she asked.

"Different generation."

"I'll say! I think we need to reduce the cabin to ashes pretty soon."

Ari and Leah walked into the house and joyfully greeted the rest of each of our families.

Joan suggested the two of them go over to Great-Grandma Esther's apartment and let her know Larry and Danielle's family had arrived.

Esther came over to the main house with Ari and Leah and greeted the rest of Larry's family with big hugs for everyone.

Leah, Ari, and Esther sat down at the table and opened some of Esther's canned nectarines and laid out some fresh-baked cookies. "Great-Grandma Esther," Leah said, "I've been looking forward to talking to you. Joan told me you knew who your life partner was the first time you met him. Can you tell me how you knew?"

"I can only tell you how it was for me. I was a little older than you two are when I met Manny. He rescued my sister, Shifrah, and me from some bullies. Although, he always insisted we rescued each other." Esther smiled at the memory.

"Manny walked us home after he scared those bullies off, and we talked about things that were important parts of our lives. It was obvious we shared many similar things, including values. I saw how my sister reacted to him in such a positive way. Mostly, I felt a growing feeling in my heart my future should be with Manny. *Kinder*, he took such good care of me. Certainly there were times when we disagreed but in all the years we were together, I never once felt I wanted anything other than a life with him—and if he became angry or I became angry, we didn't stay angry."

She looked seriously at Leah and Ari. "I'll tell you something else about us you might consider. We promised each other we would never go to bed angry at one another. Sometimes he needed some time on his own to think through a problem he was experiencing. So I left him alone during those times. He would work it out and I would have my happy, loving Manny back. It's not always easy. Sometimes one partner grows faster than the other, in a maturity sense. But be patient and soon enough you'll be at the same level again. Being together also means being supportive. Manny couldn't draw a thing but loved to watch me paint. He became filled with joy from my joy. I see that in you two as well."

Ari and Leah were holding hands under the table as Esther was talking. I'm sure they thought no one could see them as we were gathered in the other room. But with a clear view of the dining table

Joan and I saw everything. It made my heart smile. When Esther would mention some characteristic of a couple who were meant to be together, if Ari and Leah had already experienced it, Leah seemed to squeeze Ari's hand tighter as if to say, "That's us!"

Esther's expression seemed filled with remembrance of things past and hopes for the young ones' futures. "I have had a feeling for a long time the two of you belonged together. But it doesn't matter what I feel. What matters is what your heart is telling you. Leah, he looks at you like Manny looked at me. And Ari, it gives this old lady such joy to see how you watch out for her, just like Manny did for me."

After a moment of quiet Esther stood and smiled. "I have something for you at my apartment. Please come over and let me show it to you."

So the three of them walked to Esther's apartment—Ari and Leah each holding onto one of Great-Grandma Esther's hands.

Before long they returned carrying an old painting of clouds. "That's the painting I did for Manny the day after he rescued me," Esther told us. "Although I'm going to put a sign on it now, I wanted everyone to know, so there'd be no mix-ups. When I'm gone, this painting goes to these two." She gestured to Ari and Leah who were both grinning. "I know I'm old, but when I watch these two, it's like watching Manny and me when we were young."

Ari looked at Great-Grandma Esther. "Are you sure you want us to have the painting, Grandma?"

"Ari, you and Leah are more like Manny and me than anyone else in the family. You can't imagine what joy it gives me that you two are together. Even so, don't neglect your relationship. Keep it growing, and you will get more out of life than you can imagine."

"Grandma, thank you so much for leaving the painting to us. We will always treasure it," Leah promised as she hugged Great-Grandma Esther.

• • • •

AT LUNCH LEAH TOLD us she loved sailing, and Larry mentioned she was one of the top sailors at their sailing club in Florida.
"We have a Pearson Ensign at the dock. My dad says that it is
great for beginners. You can teach me," Ari immediately suggested to
her. "I've never learned to sail."

"No problem," an excited Leah replied.

Joan and I looked at each other in amazement. I had repeatedly
tried to get Ari interested in sailing, but he was only interested in
motorized craft. Until today, of course, when he discovered Leah
loved sailing.

The twenty-two-foot Ensign was perfect to learn on. It was quite
stable being a keel boat. It had a sail plan to allow for the precision
guidance of an experienced hand, or the clumsiness of a new sailor,
but in addition, would keep a new sailor from getting in trouble.

The two of them were inseparable all week and I noticed whenever one of them was assigned a job, the other would assist. When
Leah was asked to wash dishes the dishwasher, there was Ari helping.
I had to look twice to make sure it was my Ari who was *voluntarily*
assisting someone with a household chore.

Monday dawned cloudy, but with pleasant temperatures. I reminded Ari he was supposed to get all eight of my antique cars out
of their garage and wash the garage floor. So, Ari *and* Leah headed
out to the garage. They were both dressed in matching short-sleeve t-
shirts, denim shorts, and running shoes. Apparently they had a number of matching outfits they planned on wearing this week.

Ari drove each car, with Leah as the passenger, out of the garage
the twenty feet or so needed to clear the garage floor. But my Auburn
hadn't run in years, so Ari would have to use our John Deere tractor
to tow it out of the garage. He and Leah crawled under the Auburn
to attach tow cables to its suspension.

They decided Ari would drive the tractor and Leah would sit in the Auburn's driver's seat while steering and braking, if needed. When she stepped in the car, she stood up on the seat and shouted, "Ari, my legs are too short to reach the brake pedal."

"No problem, wait one," he yelled, jumping off the tractor and running into the garage. He returned with an armload of seat cushion foam padding which he stuffed behind and under Leah.

"How's that?"

"*Magnifico*," she exclaimed. "*Vamanos Hombre.*"

Ari slowly took up the slack on the tow cable and carefully pulled the old Auburn out of the garage. As soon as it was clear, Leah hit the brakes and with a mighty effort using both arms, set the parking brake.

They took out brooms, hoses, buckets, and mops. Periodically peals of laughter would come out of the garage as they worked. They discussed things endlessly and often sounded like they were in a heated debate, but never in a mean way. If nothing else they would end their discussions, it seemed, with agreeing to disagree.

It took most of the day for them to complete the job and put the cars back inside, but the floor of the garage was spotless. They were pretty clean as well. I think they put as much soap suds on each other as on the garage floor.

On Tuesday morning Larry, Danielle, Joan, and I rose early to go for a run. It was a bright and sunny June day, with a light westerly breeze—a perfect day for sailing. As we left our yard we saw sweat covered Leah, Ari, Austin, Ann, and Sara just returning from their run. I suggested that this would be an excellent day for Leah and Ari to go sailing.

Marsha didn't come out with any of us for a run. Larry told me she was starting to withdraw from the family. She was seeing a therapist, but in the midst of that joy filled family week, Marsha seemed to only see gloom and confusion in her world. Larry said her doctors were trying out some new medications, but nothing seemed to work. I even tried talking to her, but only received empty smiles and one-word answers.

Great-Grandma Esther, Ann, and Samantha prepared scrambled eggs, lox, and onions for everyone's breakfast. It was always a joy to watch Esther cooking. It was as if she was preparing love to give to us, instead of food.

After thanking them for a wonderful breakfast, Leah and Ari headed down to the Ensign. They were amazingly methodical in preparation for their day of sailing. After taking the cover off, they examined all the gear and pulled out life vests. They checked the fuel supply in the little outboard engine, as well as its oil level. Just when I thought they would get underway, they came back to the house.

I asked if anything was wrong.

"Nope," Ari replied. "We just need some stuff."

Off they went to the kitchen. Ari dug out a large picnic cooler and started making tuna fish sandwiches. He put spicy mustard on one side of the sandwich and mayo on the other. I saw him do this before and told him I thought it tasted awful.

Naturally, Leah said she loved the tuna sandwiches that way. Meanwhile, she put chips in a plastic bag, quartered a pickle, and put ice into the cooler to keep it at a safe temperature for the food.

Esther looked like she was in heaven, watching them prepare for their sailing adventure. She went to the pantry and found a jar of her canned peaches for them to take, as well as some of her cookies.

Bottled water and soda followed the food into the cooler, which was heavy by now. Without even discussing it, each one of them took an end of the cooler and walked down to the Ensign. I noticed that Ari always boarded the boat first and then turned to help Leah get on board.

Watching him work, Ari's muscular body reminded me of stories I heard about his great-grandfather Manny, but Ari was slimmer.

Raising the main sail on the Ensign was an easy one-person job. Not for those two. They both gripped the halyard and pulled together until the main sail was up. It was the same when raising the jib.

Leah was indeed an excellent sailor. When I left the dock, the sail boat was always under power until I was clear of the dock and other boats. Not Leah. As soon as Ari had untied all the dock lines and jumped on board, she pulled in the main and jib, neatly sailing out of the slip.

"You think they're mature enough to be out there all day like that and stay safe?" Joan asked me.

"Leah keeps Ari on an even emotional keel whenever they're together. She is quite protective of him and he laughs more around her than at any other time in his life. Look how she looks at him. Now watch how Ari looks at her, how he talks to her, and how he keeps an eye on her. The only time I've heard him get mad at her was when she wasn't paying attention while they were working in the garage and she banged her arm on a vice. He was upset that she wasn't taking care of herself. Believe me if a shark jumped out of the water to attack Leah, I assure you the shark would only be suitable for sushi by the time Ari finished with it. They absolutely will be safe."

Joan turned her attention to Grandma Esther. "It's amazing," she said. "I fight with Ari to get anything done, but when Leah asks it's sure, Leah, or right away, Leah—and always in a pleasant tone of voice. He had one of his mood swings when Austin made a joke about his love of engines. Ari was ready to take Austin's head off, but Leah put her hand on Ari's arm and he calmed down immediately then ignored the teasing. And sometimes I've worried that Ari was so focused on what he wanted to do, that he would never be concerned with someone else's feelings. Now I think he was saving all his compassion for Leah."

Joan watched through the window as Ari and Leah finished their last-minute preparations. "You know, Grandma," she sat down at the table beside Esther, "Larry and Danielle told me that Leah is their most obstinate child. She does what she wants to do and the consequences be damned. Ari is the same way. But get the two of them together and they cooperate and problem solve like they were perfect children. They laugh so much sometimes I think that laughter's real name is Ari and Leah"

• • • •

AS SOON AS THE ENSIGN moved away from the dock, Leah taught Ari how to tend the jib.

"Leah," Ari asked," do I pull the Jib in tight?"

"Not tight. When I show you about different point of sail, the jib position will change."

She asked Ari about it, and he told her it was a device that he and I designed and built for his cousin, Jonathan, so he could come on the boat and enjoy sailing.

"We had to make a couple of versions to get it right," he'd said. "The first version I was calling, Jonathan's Instant Sailor Bracket. But I had the back shaped all wrong, so when Jonathan tried it, he laughed and called it Instant Sailor Misery. We reshaped it and the next sunny day we could hardly get him out of the sailboat. He *loved* sailing."

Back out on the water, Leah was teaching Ari how to watch the wind and manage the main sail and tiller. He looked quite happy, having so many things to keep track of. And Leah; she was just happy. While sailing down the lake from the dock in Kirkland, Ari was piloting the boat and Leah was sitting adjacent to him while she tended the jib.

"So, what do you think of sailing?" she asked him.

"Well, aside from the gentle sound of the water lapping against the hull, the peaceful movement of the boat knifing its way through the water, the cool breeze and warm sun, the marvelous sight of our

sails against the blue sky, being powered silently by the wind and sunshine, and the opportunity to share this with the warmest, prettiest,
and brightest girl I know...I guess it's okay."

"Just okay?" she teased.

Without taking his left hand off the tiller, Ari put his right hand
on the back of Leah's neck, pulled her face toward his and kissed her

Her eyes still wide, she stared at Ari in surprise. "You should
know. I've been waiting all my young life for that kiss—and believe
me, it was worth the wait."

Ari pulled his face a small distance away from hers, smiled, and
kissed the tip of her nose.

As the sun became low in the afternoon sky, it started to cool off.
Leah grabbed a blanket and wrapped it around her and Ari. After another hour of sailing, wrapped up in the blanket and leaning against
each other, they decided to call it a day. They docked the little Ensign
and tied her up to the slip then took down and stored the sails.

Nathan and Samantha came down to the dock and asked how
the day of sailing went. Ari and Leah both confirmed they'd had a
great time and Ari said he couldn't wait to go sailing again. Nathan
and Samantha offered to help with anything, and were told they
could grab the cooler.

• • • •

BEFORE ARI GAVE HIS *Bar Mitzvah* speech the Rabbi told us he
knew Ari was quite goal oriented, and when Ari put his mind to it,
he could learn anything he wanted to.

The Rabbi made this statement because Ari was doing so poorly
in his preparation for his *Bar Mitzvah* the Rabbi was nearly ready to
call it off six weeks earlier.

When I learned how far behind Ari was, I'd talked to the Rabbi
and assured him Ari would be completely prepared by the time of his
Bar Mitzvah. With my, let's call it encouragement, Ari learned five

months of material in six weeks. Apparently only Joan and I thought he could get it done.

The Rabbi was amazed Ari could learn so much in such short a time. When the pressure was on and he had to learn a lot quickly, it almost seemed easy for him.

During the summer after sixth grade, Leah and Ari decided to read *Centennial*, by Michener. Leah was amazed how quickly Ari had read the book and then could quote different parts of it when they discussed it. It puzzled her no end that he didn't like school—except math, of course, because my encouragement would have been impossible to live with if Ari didn't do well in math.

After Ari's discussion of the day's *Parsha* at his *Bar Mitzvah*, he told the assembled, "I would like to thank the Rabbi and Cantor who guided me through my *Bar Mitzvah* preparation. I would like to thank my family for all the encouragement I received to complete my *Bar Mitzvah* studies. A special thanks to my sister, Samantha, who started the Kids Don't Belong in Wheelchairs campaign that became my *Bar Mitzvah* project as well."

The Rabbi appeared rather surprised when Ari read an additional line he had apparently secretly added at the end of his *Bar Mitzvah* speech.

Ari looked right at Leah and said, "Lastly, I wish to thank God, who puts partners in our lives that lift us when we're down, share the joys of our successes, and have such insight into our character that they can easily remove anger from our hearts and replace it with peace and joy."

Leah was beaming at him while he spoke that final line, and Great-Grandma Esther was beaming at both of them

Chapter Twelve ~ The End of an Era

AS THE DAYS AND WEEKS passed, Joan was in the habit of calling Esther's apartment around eight thirty every morning to see if she was okay.

Then, a week after Ari's *Bar Mitzvah*, Joan called and didn't get a reply. Meyer asked her if she wanted him to go check on Esther.

"No. I'll do it."

"She mentioned she hasn't been sleeping well. She's probably just sleeping in a bit today."

Joan forced a smile and said yes, then she rushed over to Esther's apartment to see if she was okay.

Joan entered and called out for her grandmother as she wandered toward the bedroom. She found Esther still in bed with her eyes closed. Joan's heart jumped into her throat as she rushed to the bedside and placed her hand on Esther's shoulder. "Grandma?"

Esther's eyes slowly opened and Joan exhaled the breath she was holding. "Grandma, I was worried when you didn't answer the phone. How are you feeling?"

"I'm feeling a little tired, dear, and weak, but I'm not in any pain."

"Let me go call the doctor," Joan offered as she turned to get the phone to call for help.

Esther reached out and placed her hand on Joan's arm. "No, dear. Just sit with me a bit and hold my hand."

"But, Grandma—"

"Sit, dear, please,"

Joan reluctantly smoothed the bedspread and took a spot on the bed beside her grandmother. As she looked into her grandmother's eyes, she felt fear and worry.

"You and Meyer have been so good to this old lady. I couldn't have asked for more. You know, near the end of his life, Manny's father thanked Manny and me for being so good to him. He'd said God would see to it that one of my children would do the same for Manny and me. Sadly, my Manny didn't live long enough to know it would be our granddaughter and her blessed husband, Meyer, who would allow me to make my senior years so fulfilling." She smiled weakly and Joan did her best to smile back.

"I couldn't have done half the things I accomplished in my old age, if I wasn't living with you. I was joyfully included in every family event. I never had to miss anything, because somehow, there was always someone available to drive me anytime I needed a ride. You even let me help you in your own kitchen. I never felt like I was in the way. Joan, you always made me feel needed. You would always point out when a dish you served was my recipe. When you're my age, you'll know how important that is."

"Grandma, it was nothing."

"My beloved Joan, it was everything. Even when it came to money, you and Meyer took such good care of my investments I never lacked for money, and as a result of your hard work, I will be giving each of my great-grandchildren a college fund."

"Grandma Esther, it's been an honor and one of the greatest joys of Meyer's and my life, to have you here with us."

"Someday, Joan, God will do the same for you and Meyer."

Joan's eyes flooded with tears, but she blinked them back, trying to latch onto some of her grandmother's calm demeanor.

After a brief pause Esther continued, "I know how close you are with Samantha, but I also know in my heart Ari and Leah will take care of you one day. You'll see."

Esther closed her eyes and Joan began to fear the worst. She sat with Esther in silence, afraid to speak and find out her beloved grandmother was gone. Then all of a sudden, Esther's eyes opened and she smiled a huge, peaceful smile. "Look, Joan—it's Manny. I can see him. Look how he's smiling at me. Oh Joan, his smile still makes me feel so good."

Esther spoke again. "Oh, Manny, it's so good to see you. So good. I've missed you, my love...yes, I'm coming."

Joan held her hand and watched, as her grandmother's breathing became shallower. She could see from the serene look on Esther's face that with thoughts of her beloved Manny on her mind, she wasn't afraid.

Esther closed her eyes, "Manny..."

Joan felt Grandma Esther's hand release its grip on hers as she quietly slipped away.

Finally, the tears building in her eyes washed down Joan's cheeks like a waterfall. She placed both her hands on her grandmother's clasped hands. "Good-bye, Grandma Esther. Say hi to Grandpa Manny for me."

Joan sat and gazed around the room that had been so filled with life and now suddenly felt so empty, her sadness tempered by the knowledge Esther had led such a fulfilling life. Still, Joan felt a pain in her heart that she hadn't felt in many years—not since she'd lost her parents in that terrible accident. She sat there and cried, not wanting to let go of Esther's hand, until she felt there were no more tears, and then she called Meyer to tell him Esther was gone.

Chapter Thirteen ~ Leah's Bat Mitzvah Week

IT WAS WONDERFUL TO see all of the Shapiro family again during Leah's *Bat Mitzvah* week in Florida. I was also excited to see Michelle and her husband Morris Kaplan and their six-year-old identical twins, Ethan and David. Michelle still referred to me to as her "big brother" and, I was quite proud of that.

We quickly caught up on each other's lives. The Warshawskys, Michelle and Danielle's parents, were in good health. With their beloved son-in-law, Larry, running the family business, they had the time to be involved in many charities as well as being on the board of the local symphony. They were busier in retirement than they were before they retired.

We arrived in Ft. Lauderdale after lunch on Sunday. By mid-morning on Monday, we were all getting ready to drive down to the Everglades. Ari always had difficulties getting acclimated to hot weather, and Florida's tropical June heat was causing him headaches. When this happened, he would take aspirin, sleep most of the first day, and then usually feel fine.

He was staying behind at Larry's house instead of going on the Everglades trip. Leah announced, "Ari is sick from the heat and I'm going to stay with him."

Joan told her, "He'll feel bad if you miss seeing the Everglades."

"And if I was sick, do you think Ari wouldn't stay behind to take care of me?"

We adults didn't seem to know what to say, but my beloved Samantha did.

"Of course, you should stay. Take good care of my brother," She told Leah and began herding us toward the door.

Joan looked at me and gave me a big smile that I knew meant, "That's our Samantha."

When it comes to sensing other people's feelings, she is the best, but I still wasn't too sure. Then I thought back to the time when Joan and I were their age. I was certain I would have wanted to do the same thing for her. Honestly, I think those two feel closer to each other and more responsible for each other than Joan and I did at that age.

I mentioned my thoughts to Joan who assured me, "They'll be fine."

• • • •

THE EVERGLADES WERE fascinating to those of us from the Northwest. The creatures and terrain seemed positively otherworldly. Although Ari and Leah's presence was missed, we all enjoyed the outing.

After we arrived back to Larry's, as day turned into evening, a cool ocean breeze came in from the Atlantic. Ari felt much better with the cooler air so he and Leah took Michelle's twins for a walk. The twins adored Ari from the first moment they met him when Ari introduced himself as Schlep Kavorkapich.

"Kavorkapich?" Ethan said, slowly repeating the name. "That's not a real name."

"Okay, Fred," Ari teased.

"Hey, you're silly," David shouted.

"Silly?" Ari yelled and picked David up, putting David's little nose against his nose and saying, "I'm certainly not silly."

"Yes, you are," Ethan giggled. Ari lowered David to the ground, picked Ethan up, and talked to him nose to nose. Playing right along as if they planned it, Leah picked David up and talked to him nose to nose too. The rest of the week, one or the other of the twins would insist on being talked to "nose to nose." They never tired of the game, while Leah and Ari never tired of picking them up.

At one-point Michelle told the twins they were being too noisy so they turned to Ari and asked him if they were being too noisy. He replied they needed to be more serious and he made a silly serious face while putting his hands on his hips. The twins, of course, imitated him.

Ari told them they weren't serious enough and they had to stand on one foot. The giggling twins followed Ari's lead and stood on one foot. When Ari started rocking forward and backwards, as if he was losing balance, finally falling forward onto the floor, the twins, laughing hysterically, collapsed on top of him.

And that's how most of the week went. Ari, the twins, and Leah seemed inseparable, and the twins absolutely minded what they would tell them—there was always the threat if they didn't do what they were told, they wouldn't be allowed to spend time with Leah and Ari.

On Tuesday morning we went to an incredible water park. Leah and Ari took care of the twins and I don't think they went on more than a couple of rides for themselves. They seemed to be perfectly happy watching the twins enjoy their activities.

"Look how happy my twins are," Michelle said to Danielle. "They've practically attached themselves to Leah and Ari. I was worried they might not have anyone else in the family to do things with, but Ari and Leah are like a big brother and sister to them. Just like Ari's dad was for me." She looked at me and smiled. "Right, big brother? You really were so good to me during those high school years."

Michelle turned back to her sister. "I heard Leah and Ari ask Morris if they could take the twins sailing tomorrow. I was nervous at first, but when Morris showed me how the twins absolutely do what they are told by either Leah or Ari, I knew it would be fine."

"Yes, they do what their told," Danielle added, "especially when Ari uses that stern tone like Meyer would use when you or I were acting childish."

"How well I remember that sound," Michelle said laughing.

Michelle smiled as she told us she was looking forward to having some time alone with Morris for the first time in a long time when Leah and Ari take the boys sailing.

The next day was sunny and warm—perfect Florida sailing weather. The twins looked adorable dressed in matching t-shirts and water shoes. They wore hibiscus covered swim suits—red for Ethan and blue for David.

Leah walked confidently around Larry's Midshipman thirty-six-foot sailboat with the twins, reviewing safety rules and teaching them the names of the various parts of the boat. They laughed themselves silly when she told them that the toilet was called the head on a boat. And they collapsed became hysterical as Ari explained the origin of the name.

Ari and Leah raised the sails, and sailed out onto the busy intra-coastal canal then into the Atlantic.

After the sail, on the walk home, the four of them stopped to have lunch at a small outdoor cafe. Ari and Leah told us the twins could hardly finish eating as they were so tired after the morning's sail in the bright Florida sunshine. By the time they walked the few blocks to Leah's house, Ari was carrying sleeping David and Leah was carrying sleeping Ethan.

They told us they had a great sail and the twins' behavior was impeccable as they performed various sailing duties while Leah or Ari manned the helm. They let the twins take turns at the wheel and Leah showed them how to coil lines and tie a few knots.

Ari apparently taught Ethan and David a few phrases so they could talk like pirates. As soon as he set David down, he woke up shouting, "Flim-flam the boson's bottom!"

A sleepy Ethan woke up, rubbed his tired eyes, and asked, "What does that even mean?"

Ari grinned from ear to ear. "Who knows? All I know is if you say those words, you'll sound like a pirate."

For the rest of the week, the twins would occasionally look off into the distance, and with one hand on their hip and the other shading their eyes, they would lean forward and yell things like flim-flam the boson's bottom, or a-vast there, you salty caterwauling poltroons, or keelhaul Aunt Betty's combat boots. This was followed by hysterical laughter from the twins and the rest of us, who couldn't resist their infectious laughter.

Once the twins calmed down sufficiently, Leah took them aside and told them, "You are learning to become real sailors. We are so proud of you."

The twins were glowing and thanked Ari and Leah for taking them sailing and for lunch.

As Danielle, Michelle, and Joan watched Ari and Leah carry the twins into the house and lay them down for a rest, it was impossible to tell which of the three of them were prouder.

After filling us in on the rest of the excursion, Ari and Leah found books to read and went out onto the shaded deck behind Larry and Danielle's home. Joan watched through the window as they sat on a long rattan couch to read—their feet touching, she noted.

I grabbed my own book and headed out to enjoy the beautiful weather for myself just as Michelle went out on the deck and told Leah, "I want you to know how much I appreciate all you do for Ethan and David, but I don't want you two to miss doing things because you are spending so much time with them."

Leah looked at her aunt and then at Ari, who was concentrating on his reading and seemed to be ignoring them. She smiled and said, "Aunt Michelle, Ari and I adore the twins, and believe me, Ari doesn't do things he doesn't like to do. Except if I ask him, of course.

But it was Ari who suggested taking them around the water park and taking them sailing. We both get so much out of watching them have fun. And don't worry, on Friday morning Dad is going to take some of us out on his new Magnum boat and he's going to teach Ari how to drive it. Believe me, it will be the highlight of Ari's trip. Besides, Ari and I are happy, as long as we are doing things together."

"You sound like your mother talking about your dad," Michelle told her.

That made Leah smile. "Aunt Michelle, when I see how happy you and Uncle Morris are, how happy my mom and dad are, and how happy Joan and Meyer are, I desperately want Ari and me to end up that happy."

"Be patient, Leah. The two of you are still young."

"I know—but when Mom tells me she knew Dad was the one for her when she was selling paintings at a mall, I think there is hope Ari and I are meant to be together. I mean, you and Meyer knew you weren't. He still feels close to you, but big-brother close."

"You're right, Leah. I just don't want you to get your hopes up and then find out the relationship isn't going anywhere."

"Aunt Michelle, would you please tell me how you met Uncle Morris."

Michelle happily told us the story of how she met Morris, and with her blessing, I shall tell it to you in her words.

Chapter Fourteen ~ Michelle and Morris

I WAS TWENTY-SEVEN when I met Morris and I was beginning to believe I would never find anyone. Here I was, a proud PhD candidate and along came this young-looking guy with wild, curly hair and a scruffy beard. His body had all the shapely attractiveness of a fire plug. He wasn't much taller than I was...but he had the most intense deep brown eyes. He stopped at my lab table and was looking over my work. Without so much as introducing himself he said, "You're not going about this correctly."

I gave him what I'd hoped was my angriest look and said, "Listen, young man, I've been a grad student for three years and I know what I'm doing."

Morris smiled at me with this incredibly warm and patient look on his face and said in a quiet voice, "When you calm down, I'll be happy to help you do this correctly."

With nothing but that warm smile, he completely disarmed me. What else could I do? I apologized for getting angry. Then I asked him to show me what I was doing wrong, and of course, he was right.

"I don't know your name," I said.

"Morris, Morris Kaplan. And you are?"

I told him I was Michelle Warshawsky.

It was midmorning when he came to my table. We worked together through lunch and didn't stop until dinner time. As Morris thought that I needed to research more journal articles, we agreed to meet again the next morning in the library.

I arrived at the library about ten o'clock and Morris was already sitting at a large table with numerous books and journals on it. He immediately started showing me a number of references that I could use. From all the material he had for me, he must have been in the library since the moment it opened. I remember thinking he had knowledge of the library and how to do research like Meyer. He also had a calm quality about him like Meyer—the one Meyer displayed when I became angry or frustrated, and it always calmed me down too. Although, Meyer did that with a serious expression on his face, but Morris did it with the warmest smile.

Around lunch time, Morris announced he would be busy for a while and would be back around two thirty. And sure enough, he sat down next to me at exactly two thirty.

I told him I was concerned I was taking an awful lot of his time.

He was about to answer when a student stopped at our table. "Dr. Kaplan, could I work with you for a while? I'm getting confused about the properties of some organic polymers." Morris told the student to get a specific book from the stacks and return with it. "One of my students," he said.

"*Dr.* Kaplan?" I asked.

"Yes, I have a PhD in biochemical engineering."

"Morris, that's a difficult field"

"Not if you have a PhD in the mathematics of optimization," he casually told me.

All this time and I was thinking he's just a fellow student. "You have two PhD's?"

He just smiled and said, "Please, we have lots to do. We can talk about degrees another time."

His student returned and Morris took out his slide rule to help the student work through some problems. I'd never seen a slide rule with so many scales. Morris's explanations to his student had the student grinning and understanding within fifteen minutes, but Morris kept asking him questions until he was certain he knew the material. Then he told him to stay at our table and gave him a few problems to work through to reinforce what he had just learned.

As the student began to work through the problems, Morris picked up one of the journals I had and walked over to the periodic index.

His student looked at me and said, "Dr. Kaplan is the best. I was nearly ready to give up on my master's degree in organic chemistry, until I took one of his classes. Nobody explains science like Dr. Kaplan. If he's helping you with your paper, it will be a great paper. He insists we work hard in his class and he assigns a huge amount of homework, but you end up knowing the material more thoroughly compared to students who take the same classes from other instructors."

This was a side of Morris I knew nothing about even though we had been working together for the last two days.

"And he's funny," the student said with a giggle. "He'll be writing something on the board and put up a symbol or equation that's completely wrong. All of a sudden, in the middle of the lecture people start laughing because they've figured out what he's done. He makes you glad you took his class. He makes every student feel they're like his favorite student. I can't wait to student teach next semester. I will absolutely be teaching like Dr. Kaplan."

Morris came over with another journal and showed me an article that I could use.

Wednesday and Thursday went the same way except I arrived when the library opened, but there was Morris, waiting each day to greet me with that smile of his.

On Friday I was working in the lab again. Morris was sitting next to me going through some of his students' papers. Into the lab walked a tall, thin man wearing an old army parka and looking angry. It was Charlie Gold. I had dated him for about three months and broke up with him. He seemed fun at first, but I had no use for his dark side when he drank.

"Hey, you," he called to me. "You could at least return my calls."

I ignored him and kept working until he came up behind me. He put his hand on my shoulder and began to pull me backwards, saying, "Look at me, bitch."

I started to yell at him to take his hand off me when, just like lightening, little Morris uncoiled like a striking snake. It was all a blur, but suddenly Charlie's legs were kicked out from under him and his body was slammed to the floor. Morris' hand gripped Charlie's throat, his knee on Charlie's chest. Morris said something to him in a quiet tone I couldn't hear, but Charlie clearly did as the color drained out of his face. Morris stood up between Charlie and me. Charlie looked scared to death and quickly left the room.

"Thank you, Morris."

"I'm from South Boston. We don't let people talk to our friends like that. He won't bother you again."

"What did you say to him?"

"I just gave him a suggestion."

"What suggestion?"

Morris turned to face me. With a somewhat embarrassed expression, he said, "I simply suggested, if he ever bothered you again, he would have to come to my office and look through my collection of formaldehyde-filled glass jars to find his reproductive organs."

I laughed. "Morris, you are wonderful."

"No, I'm just a geek."

"Yes, you are a geek, but from now on you are *my* geek." I threw my arms around his neck and kissed him.

He blushed.

"Thank you, Michelle. You are without a doubt a wonderful woman."

He looked at the floor. Without lifting his gaze, he asked shyly, "I'm having some students over for Sabbath dinner at my place tonight. Would you like to join us?"

I replied I'd love to. We worked together another hour and walked back to his apartment, arm in arm I might add.

When we arrived in the hallway to his place, there was a strong smell of cooked fish in the air. It became stronger as he opened the door to welcome me to his home. Can you believe it? He had made gefilte fish from scratch.

"Grandma Kaplan's recipe," he told me.

A small bell rang in the kitchen and Morris announced, "Just on time, the *Challah* is ready."

I couldn't believe it—he had made a *Challah* from scratch as well.

"Also Grandma Kaplan's recipe," he said, beaming at me.

We set a lovely table for the Sabbath celebration and around six thirty, eight students arrived—six guys and six girls. They looked like they were in their late teens and obviously excited to be there. They chattered like birds at a feeder.

Morris had numerous Sabbath candleholders, so each of the girls and I could light a candle.

"Everyone, this is my friend, Michelle," he introduced. "Michelle, would you do us the honor of leading the blessing of the candles?"

Believe me I blessed those candles in the sweetest tones I could manage. We had an incredible meal, but mostly I remember how the students were so excited to talk to him. When he spoke they became quiet and carefully considered every word. When he talked about the week's *Parsha*, he had all of them making suggestions on what could be learned from it. Morris made sure that everyone's ideas were welcome. Everyone obviously felt safe expressing their thoughts.

As the meal ended, I found the girls gathered around me and the boys gathered around Morris. We girls talked about dating and men—what guys wanted and what girls wanted. We talked about the importance of communication and how to talk to men. I felt like a big sister to those young girls. Maybe I was paying back Meyer for being a big brother to me.

As the students were leaving, one of the girls came up to me and said, "Thanks for being here. I feel much better having talked to you about boys. My parents aren't great communicators, so dating is one big surprise after another for me. I hope you'll be here again so we can talk."

Out of the corner of my eye I saw Morris heard what the girl said. He was grinning from ear to ear.

"I have a feeling I'll be back," I told her, while smiling at Morris.

After the students left, we cleaned up his apartment, washed the dishes, and put the leftover food away. We sat in his living room and kept talking until after two o'clock in the morning, and we never seemed to have a moment when there was nothing to say.

Looking back, I have to tell you that it was more than talking. Each time we laughed or shared an idea, I felt closer to him. We laughed a lot, even on that first Sabbath. I felt an incredible love building in my heart. I finally said it was late and I needed to go back to my own apartment. He said he would walk with me. We put on our layers of clothing to ward off the New England winter's cold.

As I arrived at his front door, I turned to thank him for the lovely evening. He smiled that amazing smile of his. He told me he was overjoyed his students could relate to me so quickly. He also told me it was an honor for him that such a kind person would share the Sabbath with him and his students.

That was it. Off came the coat and gloves—and more than I should tell my niece about. I've been holding him and loving him ever since. Two weeks later, I moved in with him. We started planning our wedding, and we haven't had a night apart since.

Chapter Fifteen ~ Crisis at Sea

ON FRIDAY MORNING SOME of us headed to the harbor for a ride in Larry's Magnum Marine Sixty-footer. As he started the first of the CAT sixteen hundred horsepower diesels, you could see Ari's face light up. When the second engine came to life, Ari's grin broadened even more. He intently scanned the instrumentation of the engines to ensure they were both operating in the green.

Austin threw the last of the mooring lines on board and jumped on the boat. Larry told Ari to get behind the wheel and put the transmission levers in reverse and we gently slid out of the slip. As soon as we were clear, Larry told to Ari move the right transmission lever to forward which pivoted the boat to the left. When we had turned nearly ninety degrees, Ari moved the left transmission lever into forward. We slowly motored out of the harbor and into the inter-coastal canal.

Leaving the harbor and under Larry's watchful eye, Ari brought the engines up so we quickly came on plane. Ari set the engines to cruise at a leisurely twenty knots. Ari was wearing his baseball cap and his aviator sunglasses, but the most remarkable feature of his appearance at that moment was the big grin on his face. Larry told him to head for the outlet and out onto the Atlantic.

As soon as we were on the Atlantic, Larry had Ari increase the speed to a comfortable thirty-five knots and told him to follow a course of one hundred eighty degrees—straight south. He explained how the throttles and trim needed to be watched carefully and how to know when to adjust them. Ari was in heaven. I think the only thing stopping his grin from being any bigger was he didn't have a bigger face.

When we had been cruising for at least an hour, Austin was looking out to sea through his Marine binoculars when he yelled to us, "I see smoke on the horizon at one hundred forty-four degrees magnetic."

He gave the binoculars to Larry who looked and yelled, "Helm, come to one hundred forty degrees magnetic."

"Aye, Captain," yelled Ari, who seemed to be having the time of his life as he carefully leaned the big Magnum into a gentle turn, now adding the compass to his vision to bring the boat to the new heading.

They all searched desperately for the smoke, but only Austin and I could see it through our powerful binoculars. Austin told us he could see flame and he asked Ari to come to a one hundred thirty-five degrees heading.

I saw the smoke too, with flame at its base. I started opening first-aid kits and assigning duties while we manoeuvred closer to the burning boat. Samantha and Leah pulled the inflate cord on the nine-foot inflatable raft and put the oars in their oarlocks once it was fully inflated. They put a boat hook and a couple of short lines in the raft. Leah retrieved blankets and towels from the cabin. By the time she arrived back on deck, Ari was slowing the Magnum and we were only fifty yards from the burning boat. It was half under water and the fire was dying at that point. We saw people in the water waving at us.

Larry had Ari rotate the Magnum so its swim platform was closer to the survivors. He and Austin launched the inflatable. It looked like two adults and three children were in the water. All of them seemed to be conscious, but appeared to be in a lot of pain.

I instructed Leah to stand on the front deck of the Magnum to keep an eye on the inflatable and the survivors. The Magnum's high sides made it hard for Ari to keep track of them at close range, but from the height of the forward deck Leah could direct Ari to put the Magnum in gear and slowly back her down toward the inflatable or one of the survivors.

Ann and I stood at the back of the boat on the swim platform. Larry and Austin started pulling the survivors out of the water and into the inflatable, the parents insisting their children be pulled out first. As soon as Austin touched the first of the children, she started screaming in pain.

I turned back toward the kids and said, "Burns—they have bad burns. Leah, keep an eye out for sharks."

With a few powerful strokes, Austin rowed the Avon over to our boat. Samantha placed towels and cushions from the boat's cabins on the deck and had blankets ready if needed. Ari ran to the back of the boat then helped Samantha and me bring the children through the transom. They were shivering so bad it looked more like they were vibrating; Samantha and Ari covered them with blankets. Their burned and charred skin looked terrible. Larry and Austin returned with the parents and we helped them on board.

They all had a number of bad cuts and bruises. The children had greenstick fractures, and the wife's face looked like she had gone ten rounds in a boxing match. He husband said the force of the explosion on their boat caused her to crash face first into a bulkhead.

I radioed the coastguard, telling them our position, and we would be at the outlet in twenty-five minutes. I had to mention that we were in a Magnum, because based on our position, most boats couldn't get back to the outlet that quickly.

Being a Vietnam combat veteran, I took charge of applying bandages and directing first aid. Ari confidently pitched right in as well, bandaging and splinting some of the bloodiest wounds.

Some of the injuries smelled of burned flesh, were quite bloody, and difficult to look at, let alone bandage and perform any type of first aid on.

Ari asked Leah to help, so she put on plastic gloves and assisted with some of the wound care. There they were, side by side, bandaging and helping the survivors. He just told her what to do and no matter how sick she looked seeing the bloody carnage she just did what he asked.

Ari and I kept talking to the injured parents in calm tones, trying to keep them as relaxed as possible, while Samantha and Ann did the same with the children. They were holding the children's hands while their wounds were being dressed.

Larry and Austin recovered the inflatable from the water, deflated it, and stored it. Ari and I showed Samantha and Ann what to do to try to minimize shock and further blood loss. Ann kept looking at the mom's battered face, and she started turning pale. Ann ran to the rail, and started vomiting. Austin went over to his sister and put his hand on her shoulder.

She waved him away, saying, "Take care of them. I'll be okay."

Larry barely finished saying they needed to get to a hospital as quickly as possible, when Ari immediately yelled, "Aye, Captain."

I turned toward Ari just in time to see him get to the helm, turn his baseball cap backwards, place the transmissions in forward, and smoothly advance the throttles of the twin CATs. The mighty diesels went from idle, to deep rumble, to full throated thunderous roar. As the boat gathered herself under the force of thirty-two hundred diesel horsepower, Ari adjusted the trim and the boat moved out at what Larry later referred to as "ludicrous speed."

I tried to yell to Ari to go gently, but my words were swallowed by the constant thunder of the twin CATs. Under the direction of Ari's capable hand, the big Magnum raged forward through the sea. As she gained speed Ari kept adjusting the throttles and trim until we were doing fifty-five knots. The mighty Magnum knifed its way through the water, smoothly splitting the ocean's swells. This allowed Ari to keep us on a smooth, laser sharp course to the outlet. Austin called out small adjustments to our heading which Ari complied with.

I smiled as I watched Ari's careful piloting of the high-speed boat. Then I looked at Larry and said, "Quick learner and one hell of a boat pilot."

"Like his dad," a grinning Larry added.

Ari was in his driving zone. He put one hundred percent of his concentration into the high-speed driving of the Magnum. With one hand on the throttles and the other on the wheel, he was all business getting the boat to a hospital.

While Ari was driving, Leah sat next to him on the wide helm seat, careful to avoid getting in his way.

The coastguard called and told us a police boat would meet us at the inlet and we should follow it to a dock where ambulances were also waiting. As we approached the inlet, Ari started bringing the throttles back to slow down for our entry. A police boat with three huge outboards was waiting, Ari maneuvered the Magnum behind them, and we cruised at about thirty-five knots to a large dock where paramedics were waiting. As the Magnum came to a stop, the paramedics jumped on board and starting treating the survivors.

As they watched the paramedics, Larry had his arms around Samantha and Ann. Even big Austin looked horrified, as the survivors were loaded on stretchers. Ari and I were only too happy to assist the paramedics.

Leah understood that my experience in the army prepared me for such things, but she didn't seem to know how Ari developed the confidence to do what he did. I wondered a bit too. She asked Ari about his calm take-charge abilities.

"We had a lot to do. I noticed years ago that my dad stayed calm in emergency situations. Whether he was calm or not, he wouldn't expose his feelings, probably because he thought exposing them might compromise the job he had to do, or in this case would frighten the survivors. Besides, you did great. I didn't see you showing how you felt."

She assured Ari that she felt sick to her stomach looking at the terrible condition of the survivors but because he stayed so calm, she forced herself to stay calm as well.

He smiled at her and said, "I know. I was watching you. You did exactly what I asked. You are one fine lady. You set your feelings aside and did what was necessary to treat the survivors. I am so proud of you."

"Thank you Ari," she said and kissed his cheek.

I decided it was a good time to tease them a little. "What?" I asked in mock surprise. "I performed all that first aid and Ari gets kissed?"

Leah walked over to me and kissed me on the cheek. "You did great, too."

As we slowly cruised back into the harbor, I told everyone what they had accomplished was a good deed—a real *Mitzvah*. "From eagle-eye Austin to everyone's help at the scene, you guys did great."

Larry added, "I am proud of each and every one of you, too."

There we stood, two former college roommates, now proud fathers, grinning at our children— proud of what they accomplished. I nudged Larry with my elbow and said, "We did good raising these clowns."

He grinned and nodded his agreement.

Once we gathered at the house I explained to the kids, "Sometimes you might relive the emotions you felt during the rescue and you may feel sad or get sick again. Take it from a combat vet—these feelings are normal. It helps to tell someone else how you feel. Not everyone reacts the same way in these situations, so don't feel bad if you think you are reacting differently than anyone else."

An hour later, Ann looked like she was about to start crying and she walked off toward her room. Leah followed and I knew she would be strong for her sister.

• • • •

AT DINNER ON THURSDAY night, I announced that the following summer my family and my nephew, Nathan, were going to take the inside passage to Alaska on a three-month boat cruise.

Leah looked sad until she noticed Ari had a huge smile on his face. She looked to me; I also wore a silly grin. "Leah, would you like to join us?" I asked.

She beamed at Ari and yelled, "Yes, I would. Thank you!"

"Leah, maybe you should check with your parents first?" I suggested, knowing I had already done so.

She looked at her dad who told her in a stern tone, "You'll be stuck on a small boat for a long time, with these people."

Leah, staring directly in Ari's eyes, said, "I can manage it."

Larry laughed. "Of course, you can go. Your mother and I already discussed it with Meyer and Joan."

We all enjoyed the rest of the week together, as we always did, and Leah's *Bat Mitzvah* was a wonderful celebration. Her project, combined with Ari's, brought in a hundred and eleven thousand dollars for research into neuromuscular disease.

After expressing her appreciation to those who helped in her *Bat Mitzvah* preparation she said special thanks, "To Samantha Minkowski, who started the Kids Don't Belong in Wheelchairs campaign that became my *Bat Mitzvah* project. Thank you for the inspiration and guidance."

Then, looking directly at Ari, Leah ended her *Bat Mitzvah* speech nearly quoting the final lines of Ari's *Bar Mitzvah* speech, saying, "Lastly, I wish to thank God, who puts partners in our lives that lift us when we're down, with whom we can share the joy of our successes, and have such insight into our character they can easily remove anger from our hearts and replace it with peace and joy."

Chapter Sixteen ~ The Inside Passage

THE FOLLOWING SUMMER, our trip up the inside passage to Alaska was under way. We'd just let customs on the Canadian side of the passage. It would be an interesting trip for Leah and Ari as they discovered photography a few summers ago. It became a frequent discussion topic for them. They were becoming the families' photo documentarians. Sometimes it seemed they spent more time looking through their cameras, than using their eyes.

My trawler had three bedroom-cabins, each with its own complete bath. Samantha and Leah shared one bedroom that had a bed and a couch that could be used as a bed. Nathan and Ari shared a cabin that contained two bunks, one over the other, and Joan and I slept in the master cabin.

The main deck of the trawler had a large living room and dining area that easily seated ten people. At the forward end of this living area was the kitchen with a large refrigerator, Viking stove and oven, a microwave, sinks, prep counters, a trash compactor, and a dishwasher. Up the ten steps to the enclosed pilothouse, located at the front of the living area, were the engine controls, electronic navigation readouts, steering wheel, and radios. There was also an elevated table and settee behind the helm. It was high enough for people sitting there to see out the pilothouse windows.

I think this was Ari and Leah's favorite perch, other than the flybridge. The front deck forward of the Portuguese bridge had a small settee that would allow up to three people to sit in the breeze at the front of the trawler.

We traveled north in the company of seven other trawlers, one of which was run by the company who had organized the voyage. They had reserved dock space and side trips for our flotilla. They also provided a naturalist to accompany us and she provided fascinating details about the flora and fauna we observed. The beauty of the mountains and fjords left us all speechless.

The amount of bird life we saw was astounding. Golden and Bald Eagles were almost common, but never boring in their majestic flight. We often knew where to look for the Bald Eagles by listening for their scream.

The water we traveled through was entertaining as well, with many orcas appearing around us. Some of the other boats put out crab traps at night. Seeing as they used well-rotted chicken necks for bait, it wasn't something I was interested in doing, but we did enjoy occasionally sharing in their bounty.

Ari and Leah busied themselves as the flotilla's photographers and videographers. Some days they traveled on other peoples' trawlers to interview them and to get more shots of our trawler. They spent their evenings on the computer editing their photos and video.

Samantha had Joan's love of the outdoors, and Nathan and Samantha were continually reading about which areas we would be traveling to and how the flora and fauna would be changing. We had one of the biggest trawlers so we took up the rearmost position of the flotilla.

We arrived in one small Alaskan town on a Friday and found a small Jewish community there. Samantha made a few phone calls and found out which home was having Sabbath services. In preparation for the *oneg* after the services, Joan, Leah, and Samantha made some desserts to take to contribute to the refreshments. We all walked from the dock to share Sabbath services with the congregants, who made us feel most welcome.

The best part of all, I was able to share this adventure with Joan and our whole family. It seemed like every time I looked at her, she was smiling over some new scenery or wildlife. Even though we made this trip before, when Samantha was young, Joan was just as excited to travel the inside passage again as she was on our first trip. Occasionally I would catch her just looking at me and smiling.

"Why are you smiling?" I would ask.

"You know," is all she would say.

I did know, as I felt the same way. I was truly blessed to have Joan in my life.

Chapter Seventeen ~ Samantha Comes to Terms

SAMANTHA WAS ATTENDING the University in Seattle and living in a dorm. As a lovely eighteen-year-old with a feminine build she made a habit of running three miles every morning. She usually ran with Ari, and Leah also joined when she was visiting. When Samantha had started running, Ari and Leah were in sixth grade, but when they were older they talked it over on one of their long-distance calls and decided they should both start running as well.

"Running helps me get rid of my anger," Samantha would tell her parents. Running was helpful for Ari as well as it evaporating his seemingly constant tension.

Samantha's first-semester roommate was rarely in the room and this allowed Samantha to study in solitude. Unfortunately, she left the university at the end of the semester and Samantha was not so lucky with her second-semester roommate. She had a lame major and lots of time on her hands, so by Friday noon she was done for the week, entertained friends in their room, and played lots of loud music.

After two weeks of this Samantha decided that she needed to find someplace else to study. She called Nathan, who lived in his own apartment on the edge of campus, to see if it would be okay to visit him for a quiet Friday afternoon study time. Samantha took a backpack full of books and started the half hour walk to Nathan's apartment. She was wearing moccasins at the time, which became a huge problem as a heavy snowfall started. By the time she reached Nathan's apartment, her hair was soaked, her body was shivering inside the thin coat she was wearing, and her feet felt like icicles.

Nathan happily greeted her and welcomed her inside. He lived in a small one-bedroom apartment decorated with used furniture

Nathan and Samantha had picked out from some stores around campus. They called the decorating style "Used Seattle College." She removed her jacket and asked Nathan for a towel to dry her hair.

"My feet are freezing," she told him, as she began toweling off her hair.

"Sit down and I'll get you warmed up." He brought over a blanket she could wrap herself in. Samantha sat on an old chair and pulled the blanket around her. As she reached down to take her wet moccasins off, Nathan kneeled in front of her and removed them for her.

"Your feet are like ice."

Samantha pulled the blanket around her so the sides overlapped in front. Nathan started massaging her feet, trying to warm them up as best he could. Samantha was enjoying this when she realized his massaging her feet was also warming up another part of her anatomy.

Just as she was trying to decode these new feelings, the doorbell rang. Nathan jumped up to open the door and there stood a well-endowed, dark-skinned woman he introduced as Sophie. To Samantha's surprise the woman kissed and hugged Nathan as she entered the apartment. Nathan was obviously pleased Sophie had joined them.

"Samantha, I have something to show you," Nathan told her after introducing her to Sophie.

He showed her a letter from a Swiss university. They had accepted him into their mathematics research program. He would be studying and conducting research near Geneva.

"I'm going to complete my degree there. Sophie has been here at our university for her one year abroad and she will be returning to the same university. We already have an apartment secured for us, with the help of Sophie's parents."

Samantha couldn't believe what she was hearing. All these years she'd thought Nathan was the person she'd marry. Who was this woman who had obviously captured Nathan's heart?

Samantha must have been showing her emotions on her face because Sophie decided to walk into the kitchen, giving the two cousins a little privacy to talk.

Nathan turned to Samantha. "I know what you're thinking, Samantha. She's not Jewish."

"No, Nathan, that doesn't concern me. It's just all these years I thought it would be you and me."

"I remember watching Leah and Ari last summer," Nathan said. "I was certain they were belonged together. They would argue with each other for hours, but if one of us took the side of one of them, suddenly they both would be on the same side, defending each other. Sometimes I thought you and I were similar—but we didn't share the closeness Ari and Leah have. They always work together, as a team, while you and I support each other working side by side on our own individual projects. In my life, I need a teammate, someone who will work side by side *with* me."

Tears were forming in her eyes as she listened to Nathan. "Nathan, my mother always told me you would need someone whose thinking was at your level. I guess she was right."

"I know, and in spite of your father teaching me mathematics isn't the most important thing in the world, it still consumes a huge part of my being. Sophie's major is physics, and she appreciates my accomplishments. We'll even be able to collaborate on research. That means a lot to me. Samantha, you are an incredible woman. I can't tell you how often I've seen my parents get teary eyed when they talk about Jonathan's career as an author. The talk always ends with; thank God Samantha was in his life."

She gave Nathan a long look. "All these years you never failed to help me when I asked. When I felt depressed, I could always call you.

You listened to all my complaints, and then you found a way to make me laugh and lift my spirits."

"I remember and we'll always remain close—as cousins."

"Will you be going to your parents' home for Sabbath tonight?"

"No. They know about my plans for Switzerland and about Sophie. That's one of the reasons I'm going to Europe. I can't stand the look of disappointment on my parents' faces."

Sophie returned to the room then, and Samantha studied in silence for a few hours, absorbing the unexpected turn of events. After a while she called Meyer to pick her up so she could spend Sabbath with her family at home.

Over dinner she told them about Nathan's plans. They were as shocked as she had been.

"Dov and Cora must be horrified," her mother said.

Samantha slumped forward onto the dining table and cried.

Her mother went to her and slipped an arm around Samantha's sobbing shoulders.

"What's this about?" Ari asked his father.

He explained. "Apparently Nathan didn't feel the same way. Samantha has been planning her whole life around the idea she and Nathan would be together. Now she has to make new plans. This will be difficult for her. It's like losing someone close to you, but they're still alive."

Chapter Eighteen ~ A Sad Farewell

SHORTLY AFTER ARI'S sixteenth birthday, I received a phone call from Larry. I could hear Danielle crying hysterically in the background and Larry's voice sounded tight and controlled as he spoke.

"Marsha's gone. She took one of the cars and used it to kill herself."

Shocked, I covered the phone with my hand and looked up at Joan. Her expression spoke volumes—something awful had happened and she wanted to know but didn't want to know, all at the same time.

I whispered the words, "Marsha killed herself."

Joan gasped in horror as her hand flew to cover her mouth. I turned my attention back to Larry.

"Marsha had been seeing a new therapist for a number of months—we had such hope for her." Larry's voice was beginning to shake. "The therapist said Marsha missed her last appointment. She was reviewing her notes and became concerned because Marsha seemed to be developing suicidal tendencies. She said she might need to be institutionalized for a time and did we know where she was. Marsha had already taken the car out. Ann immediately went to Marsha's room and found an envelope on her desk. A letter inside thanked everyone for providing a loving family for her. She wrote she was sad to leave us, but her emotional pain and constant suffering was increasing and she couldn't take it anymore."

I calmly tried to reassure my friend. "Maybe she's still—"

"No. We're too late. The police came. Told us there had been an accident involving a car registered to me. They said there was a fatality involved and they wanted to drive us to the morgue so either Danielle or I could identify the body."

"We'll be down there as soon as we can, Larry," I reassured him. "Does Michelle know?"

Larry told me yes, he just called her, so I said my good-bye and immediately called Boeing Field to charter a jet for the flight to Florida. I called Morris to give him the account number so they could also charter a jet for a rapid flight from Boston to Florida. I wanted to make sure Michelle would get to Danielle as quickly as possible, knowing the two sisters needed to be together through this horrible event.

Joan sat by silently, waiting for me to fill her in on what she seemed to already suspect. Then together we told Ari, and called Samantha, asking her to get home as quickly as possible. We would be flying to Florida as soon as we could pack.

During the flight, Joan did what she could to explain to Ari and Samantha. "There is nothing you can say when a parent loses a child, except how sorry you are."

They both nodded silently.

I turned to my son. I knew he'd have questions and concerns about Leah. "She may not want to spend as much time with you as usual. Don't take it personally. She's suffered a terrible loss and may feel more comfortable with her own family. But, if she wants you to hold her, or talk to you about her sister, then holding her and listening is the most important thing you can do for her."

Ari said he understood.

Upon arrival at Larry and Danielle's house, I approached Larry with a hug, rather than the standard handshake. Samantha stood by looking quite surprised—even more so, to see we both had tear-filled eyes too, which was something she rarely saw.

Joan seemed to be in control of her emotions, at least until she saw Danielle. The two of them embraced each other and started sobbing. Then Samantha joined in, one of the women now, too.

That evening the Shapiro's Rabbi came by the house and sat with the whole family in the living room. He encouraged them to talk about their thoughts and feelings concerning Marsha and their great loss.

We tried to stay in the background and let our good friends grieve the tragic loss of one of their own.

Danielle spoke first. "We knew she was struggling, but we had no idea she was in so much pain she wanted to end her life. I've been wracking my brain trying to figure out what I could have done differently. I feel absolutely numb." She reached over to the table in front of her. "Along with the note, Ann also found this poem." She read it aloud.

Knowing Rose
The crimson rose
It silently knows your death awaits.
Your life just waiting to meet its fate
Whether peaceful or horrible scarlet.
The crimson rose knows.
Though it's silent and cannot have said
It only hopes you might pray
To live through another day
When you die the rose knows
For it weeps a petal tear
Silent to the human ear
It flows down to the earth
Where only death is found.

Danielle began to cry, and Larry eased his arm around his wife and then spoke. "I have a hole in my heart I know will never go away. I've lost my precious little Marsha. She was jolly and happy as a preschooler, but as she grew..." his normally happy face turned pensive, "...so did her sadness. We called off her *Bat Mitzvah* because she wasn't sleeping, lying awake worrying about making mistakes in front of all our family and friends. It was just too much pressure."

Ann spoke up, a heart-breaking look on her face. "She gave me a drawing yesterday that I gave her when I was in fourth grade. She told me I should keep it for my children to enjoy. I had no idea she was giving it to me because..." tears began to stream down Ann's cheeks, "...because she would be gone the next day. When she hugged me and left, I didn't realize she was saying good-bye." She began sobbing. Danielle reached out to comfort her.

Next it was Austin's turn, stiff upper lip in check. "This morning, before she went out, she told me I was the greatest big brother in the world and gave me a big hug. I told her she was the world's greatest middle sister—like I always do." A sad smile crossed his face at the remembrance. "Then she whispered, 'No, I'm not.' I didn't realize how serious she was." He leaned forward, placing his face in his hands.

Leah sucked in a big breath before she began. "I was on the phone with Ari when she stopped by my room this morning. She hugged me and told me to make sure that Ari kept taking good care of me. She told me because she knew—how could she?"

She stood and went to Ari, throwing her arms around his neck. Ari held her tight while she cried.

He said, "I wish I could take your pain away."

"Just hold me."

Ari's face showed incredible sadness. Leah was suffering and there was nothing he could do about it.

"You and I are so happy," Leah told Ari. "We find so much joy when we're together. I feel guilty Marsha never experienced that kind of joy. How is it fair that my world is full of sunshine, lollipops, and your love when Marsha's world was shades of gray getting dimmer each day?" She glanced down at their intertwined fingers. "So many times I tried to get her to do fun things with my friends and me. Or when you and I were together, we tried to get her to do things with us. I can't believe her last words to me were to ask you to continue to take care of me." Shaking her head now, "There she was, at the end, and she was concerned you continue to take care of me—but there was no one who could take care of *her*."

Ari brushed a few strands of hair out of her face. "I'm certain Grandma Esther and *Zaydie* Manny are holding her now. If anyone can help her find some peace, I'm sure they can."

All around, it was a sad, sad day, made even sadder by the realization from everyone Marsha really did have all the love and support anyone can...and it still wasn't enough.

• • • •

THE FUNERAL WAS GRIM. The Rabbi quoted Larry, saying Marsha finally had the peace she was looking for all her short life. I suppose it's true—at least we all hope it is.

The day after, Larry and I met with Leah and Ari on the deck outside Larry and Danielle's home. I had something to discuss, which I hoped it would give them something positive to think about.

"Leah, I know the last few days have been horrible for you. However, something has been happening with the modifications Ari and I made to allow Jonathan to go sailing in the Ensign."

She nodded her head for me to go on.

"Well, it seems a woman at the sailing club saw Jonathan sailing and wanted to know how she could buy modifications for three Ensigns located at a camp on a lake in eastern Washington State. The camp is quite busy for eight weeks every summer, providing outdoor experiences for children and adolescents with neuromuscular diseases."

"That's wonderful news," Leah said.

"The sailing club in Seattle wants modifications for their Ensign as well. They want to create a community outreach program to get disabled children safely involved in sailing. I don't have time, but if you and Ari can provide them with modifications, they will buy two additional Ensigns, plus some other stable and easy to sail sailboats like the Ensign. You and Ari will need to design and build modifications for the other sailboats as well. Are you up for that?"

Leah looked to Ari and then nodded her head. "Sure, I think so."

"This is a serious business," I reminded her. "The first thing you'll have to do is create a business plan—Joan will help you. I'm willing to finance the business if you two will commit to doing the work this summer."

I turned to Ari and he gave me a nod. "I already talked to Ari and he's willing to put in the effort, so it's up to you. Naturally you'll have to move to our home in the Northwest for the summer so you can work with Ari. I have an attorney drawing up documents to create the business. Since I'm putting up the money, I will own half and you two will own half. We thought we could name the business For-Jonathan—based on the work we did to allow Jonathan to sail."

Leah smiled, taking Ari's hand.

"Is this something you would like to do?" I placed my hand on Larry's shoulder. "Your parents plus Joan and I think it could be great for you to have something to do this summer, to stay busy and not spend so much time thinking about your family's loss. What do you think?"

Leah appeared pensive, hesitating for a moment. "What does Mom think about me moving to Seattle for the summer? I mean, it would be good for me to have something to concentrate on...besides Marsha's death." She closed her eyes and took a few deep breaths. "Yes, I think this is important and might be good for me."

Larry, who had been quietly listening, finally spoke. "If you work hard at this, you could be building a business capable of putting you through university.

She looked to Ari. "I think Ari and I should definitely do this."

"Okay, you poltroons," I said, looking at the duo. "Here are the house rules. Leah, you will have your own room. If we find out you and Ari are having sex, you will be on the next plane home, and when the families get together, you two will be forbidden to come with until you are both eighteen. The two of you know me well enough to know if I tell you this, it will absolutely happen."

Ari didn't look surprised, and Leah looked like she had absolute belief there would be no compromise.

"Meyer, you are so much like Dad, and I have no doubt you and Joan only want the best for me and Ari. I will be away from home, but you and Joan should treat me like I'm one of your own," She shrugged. "Like you always have. Ari and I will stay in control of ourselves. I can't imagine not being able to see him until I'm eighteen."

"Do we have an agreement?" Larry asked.

Ari and Leah both nodded excitedly.

"Joan and I, along with your parents, have agreed any profits made go into investments for a college fund you won't be able to touch until you're eighteen. If the business makes enough money, you might get an allowance, but the amount will be agreed upon by both sets of parents and you will get equal amounts. I'm not taking any money out of the company. If you build it up, like I think you can, I will sell you my share in five years. Believe me; you won't be making any money for at least a couple of years depending on how you promote your business."

"Also, Leah," Larry said, "on a separate matter, Cora Warshawsky's brother, Dr. Isaac Rabinowitz, is a professional psychologist and specializes in family and grief counseling. I want you to know, if you need to talk to someone outside the family about Marsha's death, he's agreed to talk to you. It will be your choice, but it can be a good idea. Isaac has already talked to your mom a couple of times and she's going to see a grief counselor in Miami who Isaac knows."

Leah agreed if she felt she needed it, she would talk to Dr. Rabinowitz.

The following day we flew back to Seattle with Joan still concerned about Leah's emotional state. But after an hour in the air, she nudged me and I looked over at Leah and Ari, sitting in adjoining seats. Leah was asleep with her head on Ari's shoulder and her arms wrapped around his arm as if she was holding a teddy bear.

I agreed Leah would have some difficult times ahead, but Joan reminded me, if Ari was like his dad, Leah would be able to manage the difficult times.

Joan whispered a prayer. "Please, God, give Ari the wisdom, strength, and patience to help our blessed Leah through this difficult time."

• • • •

ARI, LEAH, AND SAMANTHA set up a routine of getting up at the same time each morning to go for a run. The rest of the day, Joan kept Ari and Leah busy working on their business. They followed strict work hours and made the base of their business in an area above the antique-car garage. They took a class in woodworking and marine finishes and started building parts for the Ensigns.

Something else happened that the family hadn't thought about. Samantha and Leah started getting close—sister close. Samantha loved cooking and especially preparing the Sabbath meal. Leah started helping the first Sabbath she was at our home and continued all summer.

They would plan the dinner, go shopping, and then cook together. Joan was in heaven watching them, and we noticed when Ari and Leah were planning a weekend activity, they would always try to include Samantha. Years later, when Samantha married, Leah would be her maid of honor.

Three weeks after the funeral, Isaac Rabinowitz came over to our home and spent a couple of hours talking with the family and then just with Ari and Leah. Leah seemed to like Dr. Rabinowitz immediately. He had a magical personal quality making him seem like he was your good friend as soon as you met him.

After talking with Leah and Ari, and with their permission, Isaac went for a walk with Joan and me, to fill us in on his thoughts.

"Whatever you're doing, keep it up. Leah feels like she can talk to you guys about anything which is emotional gold for her. Ari is obviously the rock in her life. I would give anything to see him become a psychologist, but I know what a techie he is. He has such compassion, which is especially amazing for someone his age. He feels Leah's pain and instinctively knows how to talk to her about it. When I spoke with them together, it was obvious how they support each other and nurture their relationship. I know many adult couples who don't manage as well as those two."

We agreed. Joan and I were both very proud of Ari and the young man he was becoming.

Isaac walked alongside of us, his hands clasped in front of him as he continued. "They told me instead of trying to figure out why Marsha died, they decided every week they would do something she liked to do and remember the good times with her. They said last week they ate Marsha's favorite fast food, fish and chips, for lunch one day. Another day, they went for a walk along the lake because Marsha liked to walk along the water's edge." He shook his head. "It usually takes me weeks or months of counseling to get survivors to consider doing such things, but those two decided on their own. Not only that, but I'm certain they are dealing with the loss in a healthy way, because they have already decided their first baby girl will be named Marsha."

• • • •

WE THANKED ISAAC FOR his help and returned to the house. We were so lucky to have a great clinician in the family at a tragic time like this. It was easy to see why his patients loved him.

Days passed and word about the ForJonathan business began to spread to Portland and some sailing clubs on lakes in eastern Washington and Idaho and the business continued to grow. Leah and Ari had taken pictures of Jonathan sailing in the Ensign and created a brochure they sent out to as many sailing clubs as they could find on the internet. They were getting so many requests for devices they had to contract with a woodworking shop to make and assemble some of the parts. They both worked through a text on biomechanics to create special devices for some of the physically challenged sailors.

One Monday morning, they received a phone call from an executive with a large Japanese company. While visiting Seattle on business, the owner ate lunch at the restaurant next to the sailing club. He'd noticed the Ensign going out with handicapped children and wanted to meet the business owners who produced the parts.

He came over to the house and met with us. Through an interpreter, he told Ari and Leah his son had a neuromuscular disease and he would be honored to represent their products in Japan. "Many Japanese people love sailing. I would love to take my son sailing. With your help he will sail," the interpreter told them.

As we were saying good-bye, the Japanese executive turned to me and spoke in halting English. "It must be a great honor to have children who devote their energy to helping the less fortunate."

I proudly put an arm around both Ari and Leah and agreed that yes, it was.

He turned to Ari. "Next month my wife, son, and daughter will be vacationing in Seattle with me. We will be going to museums, gardens, and baseball games. If it is possible, I would love to take my family sailing also."

A smiling Ari told him, "We can absolutely make it happen."

Chapter Nineteen ~ Ari and Leah's Next Step

AFTER A COUPLE OF SUCCESSFUL years growing the business, Leah was permanently relocating to Seattle to get ready for her college career. On Friday she would be flying in, and on Sunday, she and Ari would get the keys to the duplex townhouse they bought with proceeds from their ForJonathan Company.

On the Tuesday prior, I decided to have a serious talk with my son. "Leah is making a major commitment to live with you this year. She's a great lady and deserves the best, in my humble opinion."

Ari's face lit up at the mention of Leah. "I agree, Dad. Ever since we were little kids we had special feelings for each other and did our best to take care of each other."

"You need to consider a few things, Ari. You must be careful as there is a possibility she could get pregnant while you two are living together." By now, Ari was quite used to my direct approach to all things. "Also, it would be considerate of you to come up with a special gift expressing your commitment to her. You could give it to her when she arrives Friday."

When Friday arrived, we picked Leah up at SeaTac Airport. She was radiant and it was easy to see she was looking forward to attending university and living with Ari.

Ari too had an air of excitement about him. He planned something and he seemed barely able to contain himself until we were home. When we finally arrived he couldn't even wait until she put her bags away. He grabbed her by the hand and sat her down at the dining table.

She expressed confused anticipation, and he looked nervous and eager. "Leah, you and I have known for a long time we were meant for each other. From our first meeting, to all our family visits, I've

195

always felt I had a special relationship with you. I'm a better person because of you. Now, we're taking the next step and we are going to move into our own home and attend university together."

Joan looked on with surprise as Ari went to the refrigerator and brought out two champagne flutes, concealing them as best he could. He kneeled down and brought one out from behind his back. "I want to show you how much you mean to—"

Ari was cut off by a scream from Leah as he handed her one of the champagne flutes, which had an engagement ring tied to it with a lovely red ribbon.

"Leah, will you marry me?"

She was crying so hard she couldn't answer, so instead she threw her arms around him, spilling champagne.

When she composed herself enough to speak, she said, "You've always been so good to me."

"Does that mean yes?" Ari asked.

"Yes, yes, of course yes—a thousand times yes."

Ari untied the ribbon and placed the ring on Leah's finger and they each sipped their champagne, smiling from ear to ear.

Samantha had been waiting patiently in the background until the ring was on Leah's finger, then she began to clap and cheer.

"Were you in on this?" Joan asked.

"I helped him pick out the ring yesterday," Samantha informed her with pride, "'cause that's what big sisters do!"

Joan looked at me now. "Did you know?"

I shrugged. "Not exactly—but I had a feeling. When I saw Samantha's cat-that-ate-the-canary grin when we arrived, I knew."

Leah hugged everyone and showed off her ring. They put the phone on speaker and Ari called his Aunt Golda. She screamed for Aaron and her children to tell them the news.

Leah called her parents and Ann, her brother, Austin, and her Aunt Michelle and Uncle Morris, It was difficult for her to talk to them through her crying.

Michelle called Ethan and David over to tell them Leah was engaged to be married, and I heard one of them ask if it was to Ari.

"Yes, Ethan, who else would she get engaged to?" Michelle shouted back to him.

Then, in the background, an enthusiastic, "Yes, yes, yes!"

Michelle turned back to the conversation. "Well, David just dropped down on one knee, and punched his fist into the air screaming. I'd say it's safe to assume the twins are ecstatic Ari will officially be part of the family now. They want to speak to the happy couple to congratulate them."

She put them on the phone, coaching them from the sidelines. "Be sure you welcome Ari to our family," Michelle told them.

After the twins talked to Ari and Leah, Michelle returned to the phone, asking for Joan. "So my big brother comes through for my niece by marrying you and producing a partner for her. I am so happy for them. They always seemed like they would be perfect together, but it's so hard to know for sure. I guess they knew."

"When I think back, there were lots of signs," Joan replied. "One of the biggest was that they were always happy taking care of each other, independent of what they were doing."

Samantha smiled and expressed joy for Leah and Ari, although she seemed like she was trying not to show her sadness. I could see it. It seemed like her mother could too. Everyone else around her had a special partner, without Nathan she must have felt a little alone.

Chapter Twenty ~ A Partner for Samantha

DURING SPRING BREAK the following year, twenty-four-year-old Samantha was out with a number of friends hiking through a scenic Olympic Peninsula rain forest, located in the northwest corner of Washington State.

As they hiked along the beautiful trails, Samantha became aware of a member of the group she never met. He was quiet, a little taller than Samantha, and drop-dead gorgeous. He had a thin build like a distance runner. Samantha decided she would talk to him.

She found out he was quite knowledgeable about the rain forest. He told her it was formed thousands of years ago by glaciers, as well as many facts about the flora and fauna of the Olympic Peninsula. As they walked, they started to discuss many subjects. Samantha was quite pleased this guy was so well read. She found she was laughing with him quite a bit, as well.

Looking at the great muscle definition he had in his legs, she asked if he was a runner.

"I run at least three miles a day and try to run a five-K once a month," He replied.

"I run a couple miles every day," she told him, "but I've never run a five-K."

"Maybe we could get together for a run sometime," he suggested.

"That would be fun. What's your major?" She assumed he must be a bio major, with all of his knowledge about the rain forest.

"If I tell you, you have to promise to keep talking to me." He grinned.

She returned his smile. "I'll let you know after you tell me."

"I'm working on a PhD. I'm majoring in knots—you know, like when you tie your shoes."

"Oh really," a broadly smiling Samantha said. "Are you good enough to apply knot theory to protein folding?"

He gave her a shocked look, "You know about knot theory?"

"My dad has a PhD in mathematical optimization, as well as finance."

"What's your name?" he asked.

"Samantha Minkowski."

Upon hearing her name, his face brightened further. He looked at the necklace she was wearing—a miniature *Chai* suspended on a chain. With a knowing smile he said, "How about dinner together tomorrow night?"

Samantha replied, "I don't go out on Friday nights."

"I'm sorry. I should have said that I was asking if you would do me the honor of coming to my home and lighting Sabbath candles for me."

Oh my God, thought Samantha, *he's Jewish*!

"I'm Gould by the way, Moshe Gould."

Samantha's heart was racing as she shook hands with him and told him that she would prefer that he came to her apartment the following day. "Tell you what, Moshe. Why don't we meet at my place around four o'clock and we can walk to a market nearby. We can buy whatever looks good and cook it for dinner."

"Four o'clock sounds fine."

Driving back to the University, Samantha rode with Moshe in his slant-nose Porsche 935. She was surprised to see that he had installed four-point belts in the car. It looked more like a race car than a street car.

"I did some aerodynamic work for my father last summer and he paid me with the car. It's wonderfully quick, has great handling, but also is safe."

The ride back to the University a number of interesting discussions. It seemed they were never going to run out of things to say to each other.

When Samantha asked her friends about Moshe, they told her some people thought he must be gay, because so many girls had tried unsuccessfully to get him to go out with them.

"I guess he was waiting for you," Samantha's friend Rachel told her.

When four o'clock on Friday arrived, they walked to the market and bought a beautiful tuna filet. They took it home to marinate and then cook outside on a charcoal grill.

Moshe also grilled fresh vegetables and made a Rumanian-style eggplant dish. They shared kitchen duties, lots of conversation, and even more laughter. Moshe could act, and at times, he would tease Samantha by talking in a serious voice preventing her from knowing whether he was kidding or not.

She loved that. Naturally, his silliness provided even more opportunity for laughter.

Samantha blessed the candles to welcome the Sabbath. Moshe recited the blessing for the wine and she recited the blessing for the beautiful *Challah* she had baked for them that morning.

Before they opened their prayer books, Moshe recommended they sing the *Shehechianu* because, he said, "I feel this is going to be the first of many Sabbaths we celebrate together."

As they started to eat, he told her, "Wait until you hear the commentary by the Lubavitch Rebbe on tonight's *Parsha*. It is fascinating."

After dinner he asked if she would like to go dancing with him on Sunday evening. "Seattle has a great Lindy scene," he told her.

Samantha couldn't believe her luck. She met a great guy who cooks, *davens*, and dances. This was too good to be true.

"You're an interesting guy, Moshe. How come no one has latched onto you yet?"

"Someone did. We were about to become engaged when her parents made it clear that I wasn't sufficiently Jewish for their daughter. We were having huge arguments with them, and with each other. I thought we were so perfect—we spent four years together, from age seventeen to twenty-one—and then her parents basically told her she had to choose between her family and me."

He shrugged. "It was about control. I'm an independent guy and her parents always did things in a way to continually run her life. Having an independent guy around, who wasn't afraid to tell people what he thought, was anathema to them. She finally told me she needed time to decide. Four years together and she needed time to decide? I told her I decided—to say good-bye. I remember when I told my dad, he said, 'About time you woke up.'"

Samantha briefly described how she was certain she was intended to marry Nathan. "I felt we were perfect for each other but Nathan didn't share my feeling. My brother, Ari, found his partner at a young age. Our parents knew they were right for each other from a young age, too. I always thought the same thing would happen to me."

Moshe told her, "I've dated off and on since then. The older I became, the more I realized what I wanted in a relationship. It's so much easier now to get an understanding of a person early in a relationship. There are some key questions I ask, or subjects I bring up. Unlike everyone else I've run into, you're the only one who wants so many of the same things in a relationship I want. I don't even remember how many times we've talked about how important our families are to each of us—but that's when I realized you were someone special."

Samantha said, "Values—my wise father always tells me—values are what make us who we are. Dad told me many times the most important thing we can give our children is free—a set of values to live by."

"I'd love to meet him."

"I'm sure he'd love to meet you as well."

"I know we just met, but I enjoy your company. I felt a connection to you in the first few minutes we were together. The longer we talked, the closer I felt."

"After I lit the candles tonight and we embraced, it was hard to let go."

They moved to the living room. Samantha sat next to Moshe on a big couch, and they talked for hours. They laughed, they teased, and they enjoyed a late snack of wine, cheese, and sliced apples, feeling and acting as if they had known each other for years.

Moshe suggested that it was getting late and that maybe he should head home.

Samantha moved from sitting next to him, to sitting on his lap. She started kissing him and wrapped her arms around his neck. "Don't you dare leave. Stay with me tonight."

"I think this relationship is special, and I hesitate to do anything to jeopardize what we have started," he told her.

"Look, I'm a big girl and I know what I want. Tonight I want Moshe."

"Well you know, if I stay, we'll have to engage in the traditional Sabbath *Mitzvah*."

"Lucky me," a giggling Samantha told him.

The next morning they drove the Porsche over to Dov's home for Saturday morning Torah study. Samantha was glowing each of the many times Moshe added some insight to the discussions. He was particularly skilled at demonstrating modern relevance to the ancient stories.

Cora invited Moshe and Samantha to stay for lunch. Meyer and Moshe spent most of the lunch discussing knot theory.

Ari nudged Samantha during lunch and said to her, "Cool wheels you arrived in."

Everyone seemed to like him. She decided Moshe and her dad were going to be great friends. Even Ari and Leah were spending time talking to him. Dov nodded in approval when Moshe mentioned a life lesson Moshe's father taught him about this week's Parsha.

Her parents were ecstatic over Samantha's new boyfriend. "Like Samantha says," her mother commented to her father, "he cooks, he *davens*, and he dances. What could be better for her? I sure hope this is the one. Good thing we never burned down the cabin."

Her father burst out laughing.

• • • •

THREE MONTHS LATER, Moshe drove Samantha up to the cabin in her father's fully restored Auburn 851 Cabriolet. Moshe loved antique cars, so Ari, Moshe, and her dad shared yet another connection.

Her mother had given them driving instructions on how to get to the cabin following the same route she and Meyer had taken many years earlier. "Don't forget to stop at the farmer's market in Cashmere," her mother had told them.

As they drove next to the Columbia River, Samantha found the location where her mother and father took a self-portrait photo when they visited the cabin all those years before. Samantha asked Moshe take a photo of them, staged the same way at the same location.

They arrived at the cabin late on Sunday afternoon. The next morning, while Samantha was walking downstairs, she saw Moshe started cooking breakfast. There were champagne flutes on the table and Samantha immediately looked to see if there was an engagement ring in one of the glasses—there was—and she started screaming the word yes, even before Moshe proposed.

A beaming Samantha asked, "Why did you put the ring in a champagne glass?"

"I heard that's how it's done in your family. Your mom also said something about shooting a bear to prove my commitment to you—but your parents started laughing so hard, I didn't have a chance to ask them what she meant."

Chapter Twenty-One ~ Full Circle

SAMANTHA AND MOSHE decided on a June wedding. All the Shapiros, Kaplans, and Goulds were in town. It was amazing to see how much Michelle and Morris' twins grew since the last time we saw them. Michelle's four-year-old son, Jonah, also discovered how much fun it was to spend time with me. The little guy loved to read and he and I spent a lot of time exploring my library. He read beginner books to me and I read children's Sci-Fi to him.

Early on Wednesday morning, I took my fire-engine-red, two-seat Shelby Cobra out of the garage to show to Moshe. Michelle insisted Jonah started shaking as soon as he heard the Cobra's monster engine thunder to life, so she walked him out to the front drive.

"He was so excited to see and hear the car, I was afraid his head would explode," Michelle told us.

I parked in front of the house and was showing its engine to Moshe, when I noticed the look on Jonah's face. I picked him up so he could see too.

"Man, look at them pipes!" Moshe said.

Jonah agreed. "Yeah, look at them pipes."

I saw the look in Jonah's eyes and told him, "I have to take the Cobra out for a run to warm up the oil. Would you like to come with me?"

"Yes," Jonah screamed, barely able to contain his excitement.

Ari and I fitted a child seat into the Cobra's passenger side. Leah took some photos for Jonah to take home. We have a picture of Ari standing near the front of the Cobra when he was the same age, and it's labeled, *Ari's first love*. Leah wanted to be sure Jonah had a picture with his first love too.

I took the Cobra out onto I90 and headed east, I noticed that Jonah was watching the tachometer and studying me while I shifted gears. We talked about the car and its history and I was pleasantly

surprised at the questions Jonah asked. He wanted to know everything about the Cobra, its controls, and how they worked.

An hour and a half later, we returned home.

"What took so long?" Joan asked. "I thought you were just going
to warm up the oil?"

"We decided we needed some cherry pie," I told her with a grin.
"Naturally, we had to get the best, so we drove to that corner restaurant in North Bend. Joan, this is not difficult to understand. He's a
car guy and he needed some cherry pie."

Jonah became excited, and with pride declared to his dad, "Dad,
I'm a car guy."

"I know. I've seen it," grinning Morris told his son.

Michelle commented to Joan and Danielle, "Meyer is still my
big brother. Look how he finds time for Jonah." Then she told us
we had to get out to the driveway when the twins' two new friends
arrived. "They met at camp last summer and when the twins knew
we were coming to Washington State for Samantha's wedding, they
asked their friends' parents if they could come to Seattle for a day. So
their parents are driving them the three hours from Wenatchee. They
were planning something special for us."

When they arrived in the morning the twins were in the driveway waiting. As Michelle suggested, we all walked out to join them.
Ethan and David were wearing brightly-colored Hawaiian shirts,
Ethan wearing red, David wearing blue. I was surprised since the
boys generally didn't wear such bright colors. Both were also wearing
matching tan shorts and matching running shoes.

A full-size SUV pulled into the driveway and as soon as it came
to a stop, the right rear door flew open and the twins' friends jumped
out. They both ran to the front of the SUV and stood side by side.
Upon spotting the twins they each put their left hand on their left
hip and placed their right hand on their brow shading their eyes.
"Keelhaul Aunt Betty's combat boots," they yelled.

Ethan and David assumed an identical position and yelled, "Do that and you'll both be tied to the mast."

They all giggled, David and Ethan ran over to Megan and Sheryl, and then the four of them formed a circle with their arms on each other's shoulders, marching in place. As they rhythmically pronounced the first two words of the next saying, they opened their circle into a straight line facing the family. Together they shouted, "Alemen! Alemen! Alemen kockteple, yiskada boom, boom, you pasguniak, go right home!"

They high fived each other, and then immediately re-formed an evenly-spaced line facing the family. They came to attention, like four little soldiers. In deep, loud voices they began slowly yelling, "A-Two-Two, we are the Tigers—"

Immediately the two sets of friends were cut off by Ari and me yelling, "That's good enough. Thank you, thank you."

The twins and their friends engaged in brief hugs and ran over to meet the rest of the family.

"Did you teach them A22?" Joan asked in an accusatory tone.

"I certainly did not." Then I looked at Ari, who had little Jonah sitting on his shoulders.

"Not me, Dad," Ari informed them.

Ari in turn looked over at Leah who was grinning until she saw Ari looking at her. The smile left her face and she shrugged her shoulders, indicating she had no idea how the twins learned about A22. At that point, and at various times the rest of the week, Jonah could be heard saying proudly, "A22, we are the Tigers!"

The outfits Megan and Sheryl were wearing matched the Kaplan twins' outfits—Megan matching David and Sheryl matching Ethan. Megan and Sheryl were slim and roughly the same height as the twins, and their laughter and bright expressions made them sparkle like little jewels.

As we introduced ourselves to their parents and welcomed them into our home, Joan exclaimed, "I don't believe it. They're identical twins."

"They're our miracle twins," Mindy Cohen explained. "We tried every medical treatment known to man to get pregnant and nothing worked. Three months after we gave up on a cure, I found we were pregnant with the twins."

Leah started taking pictures while Ari talked to the Cohen twins. "So you two are the troublemakers I've heard about."

"That would be us," Megan replied with a big smile.

"There is a rumor around that the Cohen and Kaplan twins need a sailing lesson," Ari suggested.

"Oh yes, please, please, please, please," Sheryl said rapidly.

Megan proudly told Ari, "Ethan and David were the best sailors at our camp. Also the funniest. We were racing the last week of camp and they won all the boys' races. We didn't win all the girls' races, but we had the noisiest cheering section. They even cheered us when we lost. Then we partnered with them on a bigger four-person sailboat and we won a few races, but even when we lost, we had the most fun."

"One of the counselors said our sailboat was powered by laughter," David told them.

"They named it the Comedy Craft," Sheryl told us proudly.

"We have to get some things from the kitchen and take them down to the Ensign sailboat," Ari said, and the four of them raced off to the kitchen with Ari and Leah close behind.

"I have so much trouble with those two fighting with each other," Mindy told us. "It's so bad, we warned the camp counselors they should keep them in separate activities whenever possible. We didn't even want them bunking near each other. After two days of camp, we called to see how they were doing and the counselors told us they were absolute angels as long as they were with their friends. It didn't occur to us, until we saw the DVD they brought home, that their friends were twin boys. They spent all last week worrying about whether David and Ethan would be happy to see them. I'd say they needn't have worried."

"It's like watching Ari and Leah when they were that age—except double," Joan said.

David and Megan raised the main sail followed by Ethan and Sheryl raising the Jib. Ari untied the Ensign and, with Leah at the helm, they slid quietly from the dock and out onto the lake. The day was perfect for sailing.

As we stood on the dock, Robert Cohen asked me about the NM sixty-five-foot trawler. "I'd love to see it, if you have time," he said.

"We're planning a short cruise after lunch. Would you like to join us?" I asked.

"He'd love to," Mindy told us with a laugh. "You think the twins were excited to see each other? My husband gets as excited about boats."

Larry and I started talking with Robert about boating, and sure enough, he was a dyed-in-the-wool powerboat sailor. As the families watched the twins head off on their sailing lesson with Ari and Leah, I offered to take Robert down to the trawler to inspect it.

"You can show it to him, but we might not see him again." Mindy laughed. "We have a thirty-four-foot cruiser I swear he looks at with the same love as he looks at me."

"Gee—I think I know about that," Danielle said and elbowed Larry in the side. "I think his actual first girlfriend was named Connie."

Larry, Robert, and I headed down to the trawler. Robert wanted to see the engine room first, and Larry and I were in heaven showing him all the mechanical and electronic systems.

After lunch we went for a two-hour cruise around the lake. Robert spent most of the trip at the helm—which he just loved.

"Look at him," Mindy told Joan and Danielle. "I don't think he was as excited during our honeymoon."

The Cohen's were a delightful family who fit right in. Mindy's amazing sense of humor kept us laughing all day.

Just before dinner, Joan and I told the Cohen's they should return on Friday and spend the weekend with us celebrating Samantha's wedding.

Robert declined, saying, "No, we'd be intruding—you've been more than kind to us. We couldn't intrude on a family event."

But I insisted, "We're powerboat family—that's family enough for me."

Robert tuned toward his wife. "Mindy, I have to work tomorrow but I could free up Friday."

She agreed and it was decided. Mindy smiled and told us, "When we returned from the after-lunch cruise, I found both sets of twins in the library. They were taking turns reading and discussing stanzas of Shel Silverstein's poems. Ari and Leah were helping them choose poems. They were also making suggestions on how the four of them could put emotion into their reading. She's found two other books of poetry with poems she thinks the twins would enjoy reading to each other. The four of them are absolutely in heaven. It's almost like Leah and Ari are their big sister and brother."

"That's a genetic trait in this family," Michelle told them.

"Megan and Sheryl can stay with Ari and Leah at their apartment tonight and tomorrow night," Joan offered.

Mindy commented, "Well, I've haven't seen many children this age get along so well. Especially my two girls."

"I was thinking, when you come back on Friday, your family doesn't need a hotel room. You can stay on the trawler," I suggested.

"Ow, quit twisting my arm. It hurts, it hurts," Robert teased, while everyone started laughing.

After talking to Megan and Sheryl to see if they would like to stay at Ari and Leah's apartment—they did—Robert and Mindy headed home.

Before dinner the four twins performed Silverstein's poems for the assembled family. David and Ethan set up a video camera to record the readings. They seemed to be spending a lot of time on their new hobby of making videos.

The next morning after breakfast, Joan overheard Megan and Sheryl talking about how they loved gardening.

"I have two ten-foot-long flower beds near the dock I haven't had time to work on. If you would like to plant flowers in them, I will have Ari drive you over to the garden center and you can pick out whatever you like. The beds are in awful condition. You'll have to work like mad to get them in shape."

"I'm sure David and Ethan will help us," Megan said.

"They have shown no interest in gardening at our house in Boston," Michelle warned them.

David and Ethan were more than happy to garden with the girls, so Ari and Leah took them to the garden center. The boys cheerfully volunteered to implement the girls' garden design. The girls looked forward to choosing the plants.

Megan expressed a concern that no one would be around to take care of the flower beds after they went back to Wenatchee.

Ethan told them, "David and I can take turns during the week coming over to check on them."

Sheryl gave Ethan an exasperated look and said, "You'll fly in from Boston every week?"

"You haven't heard, I guess," Leah said.

Leah looked at Ari. "David and Ethan know, so I guess it is okay to tell Megan and Sheryl."

"Tell us what?" they chirped in unison.

"We had a family meeting the day before you arrived. Morris and Michelle, David and Ethan's parents, want to start a bio-tech company using algorithms that Morris has discovered. Moshe and Meyer have agreed to finance their company. Morris has no interest in running a business, so Meyer and Ari are going to run the business for them. Ari is going to take the next semester off to help them get started. Right now, Michelle and Morris are out looking at a house about three blocks from our house."

"You mean they're moving here?" Megan yelled.

Sheryl added, "Oh wow. Oh wow. Oh wow."

• • • •

THE COHEN'S ARRIVED Friday morning and they went out to lunch with the rest of us parents. They told us Robert's sales business was doing so poorly they barely make ends meet.

"It's getting hard to find companies to rep. I'm not sure what I'm going to do next."

Morris and I looked at each other in amazement.

"We need a sales guy for the company we're forming. If you're willing to learn about our business, we'll pay you to move your family here," Morris told him. "You'll be Head of Marketing and Sales, to start. We even have a budget for the first five years, so the job is secure for at least that long."

Robert and Mindy looked at each other in shocked silence.

"Moving your family here includes moving your boat," I said with a grin.

"You don't even know me,"

I asked, "Robert, are you wanted by the police?"

Mindy laughed and answered, "Not in this state."

Everyone laughed and an ecstatic Robert said, "Let's talk. Let's talk."

An hour later there were handshakes all around and the Cohen parents started planning a move to the Seattle area.

After lunch on Friday afternoon, the families decided to go for a walk in a park along the lake. Ari, David, and Ethan walked together following the other parents, while Megan and Sheryl followed a distance behind with Leah and Joan, and I brought up the rear.

"We wanted to ask you about something," Sheryl asked Leah.

"For now, holding hands and hugging is enough," Leah told them.

"How did you know we wanted to ask that?" asked Megan.

"Because I was twelve once too, and I see the four of you look at each other like Ari and I did at your age."

"If you don't mind telling us, when was the first time that you and Ari kissed?"

Leah glanced back at me, to see if we could overhear their conversation. I simply wore a neutral expression and melted into the background.

Leah blushed a little, but smiled and turned back to the twins. "We were sailing on the Ensign the week of Ari's *Bar Mitzvah* when Ari kissed me the first time. I'll never forget it."

"Really?" the twins asked.

"Yes, really. But beyond that, we waited. It was the right thing to do. For you too. Why did you ask?"

Megan began, "Last summer at camp, David hugged me a few times and it was nice, but when he hugged me when we arrived this time, my body kind of reacted in a different way. What was weird, though, is when Ethan hugged me it was more like hugging my dad."

Sheryl added, "Same thing happened for me. When David embraced me it was nice but when Ethan held me—well, it was much better."

"Look, here's why it's best to wait, you two are still young, and you don't know what the future holds. For example, Samantha spent her whole young life thinking that her cousin, Nathan, was going to be her life partner. When she was eighteen, she found out he didn't feel the same, and it was nearly another six years before she met Moshe. It may be awhile before you know."

"But *how* will we know?" Sheryl asked.

"You'll know in a thousand different ways—but mostly in your heart. For instance, it doesn't matter what Ari and I are doing, we're happy as long as we're together. Sometimes I think I know we're partners because of how we get along when life is hard—like when my sister, Marsha, died. I was an emotional train wreck."

Joan squeezed my hand a little tighter when Leah started talking about that tragic time.

"Right after," Leah continued, "our families thought I should move up here from Florida for a summer, to help Ari get our For-Jonathan business off the ground. Ari was a rock for me. Sometimes I was so depressed I couldn't do my share of the work, but he never complained. Instead he did my work as well as his own. The first few weeks living up here, I didn't want to get out of bed, but I knew Ari would be waiting for me, so I did. By the end of summer I was almost back to my usual self. I mean, I'll always feel a loss when I think about Marsha, but Ari's support really helped me get over the hardest part, and I intend to spend the rest of my life paying him back."

The three of them walked in silence for a few minutes then Leah continued, "Did you know that Ari doesn't like sailing?"

The twins looked at each other in amazement.

"That's right. He would give it up tomorrow without a second thought. Watch his face when we go out sailing again. He'll be watching me enjoy something I love. See Joan and Meyer holding hands back there?"

They all turned back to look, so I pulled Joan in closer and gave her a kiss on the cheek.

Leah smiled. "Joan loves to paint. Meyer has no interest in painting—but if you go to Joan's studio, you'll see a lounge chair with a table and lamp next to it. On the table will be whatever book Meyer is reading. It's there because he gets a kick out of watching her paint, he wants to be in the same room with her when she's doing what she likes."

"Did you see how David and Ethan worked the soil in the flower beds for us?" Megan said to Leah. "All we had to do was wait until it was ready. Then we placed the plants where we wanted them. The boys even strung out hoses and watered them for us."

Sheryl added, "And I was yelled at when I tried to move the two forty-pound bags of potting soil. I was mad at first, but then I realized they were watching out for me—protecting me. I love that feeling."

"I'll tell you a story about Ari's great-great-grandfather," Leah said. "He was a retired blacksmith whose wife died many years before and his best friend was a retired doctor. They shared a passion for peach, nectarine, and apple trees. They loved to be outside working in their orchard. Many days, the doctor's wife, Rose, would have one of the men take a chair to the orchard where they would be working. She would sit and knit, and watch them. Ari's Great-Grandmother Esther told me once, 'Rose so loved to see those two old men, working together and debating about how best to take care of those trees, she used to pray there were orchards in the afterlife for them to work on—because that was truly heaven for them.' Heaven for Rose was getting joy from what her dear husband was doing."

"That sounds nice," Megan said. "That's what I want."

"Well, it takes work to keep your relationship growing. I can only tell you what works for Ari and me. You'll have to discover on your own what works for you."

"Like what?" Megan asked.

"Like if Ari and I have a disagreement, we agree to disagree. Meyer and Joan try never to go to bed angry. My dad and mom go for a half day cruise on their antique boat every month, just to make sure they take some time for their relationship. It's not always easy to find time, but they think it's important, so they make time at least once a month."

Up ahead David and Ethan began jumping up and down and looking back at Sheryl and Megan. David yelled out, "The Comedy Craft lives."

"I think Ari may have told David and Ethan we just purchased a new sailboat. Our new boat is forty feet long and good for overnight cruises. Meyer was thinking of selling the Ensign, but Ari told him he should offer to sell it to the four of you. I think David was telling you what he thinks the name of the boat should be."

Sheryl screamed at the boys, "Yes, the Comedy Craft lives."

Ari and the boys stopped and waited for Leah and the girls to catch up to them as Megan asked Leah, "How will we pay for it?"

"Ari and Leah are going to be great parents someday," Joan said.

"I do believe you're right," I agreed and smiled as Leah explained my plans for the twins.

"Meyer says the Ensign needs to be hauled out of the water and she needs lots of maintenance. He and Ari will teach you how to do the work. I assure you, the four of you will be busy for many days this summer working on renewing that little boat. Plus, his gardener, Javier, took a new job so lots of gardening will be needed this year."

Ari warned them, "This is not all fun and games, guys and girls. There will be house rules about where and when the four of you can get together. If you don't follow them you'll be separated, lose the Ensign, and be prevented from seeing each other for a long time. When Leah came up here after her sister's death, we were told that if we didn't follow the house rules, we wouldn't be allowed to see each other until we were eighteen!"

The four twins looked at each other with serious expressions, which gradually morphed into four smiling faces.

"We can do this," said Ethan.

"It will test your togetherness" Leah added. "Some days you'll be tired and sore and not feeling like interacting with each other. The four of you will have to work at keeping up a good relationship even on days when you don't feel like it. That's the hard work I mentioned before."

"But if we're really meant to be together," Ethan said, "it will be worth the effort."

Megan and Sheryl looked at each other with huge smiles.

"Yes, I promise it will be worth the effort," Ari told them smiling at Leah. "Nothing in life is certain, but please notice God didn't just get you together at camp last summer. He brought you together again this week, and it looks like you may be able to spend even more time together. He's giving you a chance to keep your friendship growing, but it's up to the four of you to do it."

Sheryl wanted to know if Ari and Leah would be around during the summer, to help them if they had problems getting along. "Sometimes it's hard to talk to parents about this kind of thing."

"Of course," Leah told them, "We will make sure that the six of us to get together for Sabbath every week at Ari's and my place. If not at our place, then we will arrange to meet afterwards to talk about how our week went. If anything comes up, we'll talk about it together, or privately, as you wish."

It looked like Megan had tears forming in her eyes as she asked Ari and Leah, "Why are you doing all this for us?"

Leah laughed and said, "Because Meyer and Joan, my parents, Great-Grandma Esther, and Ari's sister Samantha did the same thing for us."

Ari explained, "It's our duty because other people did that for us. When you have the time, ask Ethan and David about why their mother Michelle, to this day, refers to my dad as her big brother. And you know how Jonah loves that red car. Well, my dad has already promised him he will be in front of their new home at Seven o'clock every Sunday morning this summer to take him out for breakfast in the red car. Sure, Jonah is excited about the car, but think about what Dad is doing. He's building a relationship with Jonah so years from now, when Jonah has problems he doesn't want to tell his parents about—who will he talk to? It will be easy to talk to my dad. When Leah and I were seven years old, we were at an amusement park in Florida. My sister Samantha took time out of her vacation to take us on all the little kid rides we wanted to go on. Samantha was the first one in the family to treat us like a couple. She made sure we talked and acted respectfully toward each other, even at seven years of age."

"You guys did the same for David and me when we were that age," Ethan reminded Ari and Leah.

"And someday you'll do that for someone else and that's how you'll thank us," Leah said.

Ari and Leah were thanking Joan and I, by showing what they had learned from us throughout their lives.

As we all started up the path to head back to the house, Ari and Leah were holding hands. I held my beloved Joan's hand just a little tighter, thinking Grandma Esther and *her* beloved Manny were smiling at us.

What goes around really does come around—it's true. The example that Manny and Esther set for their children trickled all the way down to what Ari and Leah were now doing for the twins.

Joan leaned into me and pulled me closer, as Ethan held out his hand to Sheryl and David held out his to Megan. It looked like, maybe for the first time in their young relationship, the two couples were walking hand in hand. Their young minds would be filled with the joy of knowing they would be spending the summer together, working together.

Just then, breaking into my pondering, Ethan yelled ahead to Ari and Leah, "Hey. What are you going to name your new sailboat?"

I could see Ari and Leah smile at each other as they shouted back to the twins, "*Bashert*, of course."

~~~ **The End** ~~~

Don't miss out!

Visit the website below and you can sign up to receive emails whenever Richard Alan publishes a new book. There's no charge and no obligation.

https://books2read.com/r/B-A-XUNH-CXYW

BOOKS 2 READ

Connecting independent readers to independent writers.

Also by Richard Alan

Meant to be Together
Finding a Soul Mate
The Couples
Finding Each Other
Growing Together

Watch for more at https://villagedrummerfiction.com.

About the Author

Richard is a 101st Airborne Division Vietnam veteran. After an education in mathematics, 17-years in manufacturing engineering then 22-years as a software engineer, Richard embarked on a career in writing. His debut series, Meant to Be Together, is a tender and heartwarming, multigenerational family saga about relationships, love and life. This was followed by a series of historical fiction novels, set in 1847 – 1900, about the predecessors to the characters in his Meant to Be Together series. Expertly researched, American Journeys: From Ireland to the Pacific Northwest (1847 – 1900), Volumes One and Two, details the family's struggles during the Great Irish Famine, emigration from Ireland to Boston, the journey across the United States, the Oregon Trail, and the Panama Canal. A Female Doctor in the Civil War follows Dr. Abby Kaplan, trying to become a surgeon during the Civil War. She was first introduced as a little girl in Volume One of American Journeys. Being a lifelong learner, Richard loves pursuing the research for his historical fiction. It is frequently accomplished while RV traveling with his wife, Carolynn, to libraries, museums, and historical sites around the country. Having a career that is portable permits traveling to many spectacular areas of the United States. It also provides opportunities to visit our adult children, grandchildren, other relatives, and friends.

Read more at https://villagedrummerfiction.com.

CPSIA information can be obtained
at www.ICGtesting.com
Printed in the USA
BVHW051135060623
665472BV00014B/1321